THE ECHO 2

# DARK BETWEEN OCEANS

BELINDA CRAWFORD

HENDRIX & FAUST
PUBLISHERS

Published by Hendrix & Faust, Publishers in 2020

Text copyright © Belinda Crawford 2020

www.belindacrawford.com

ISBN: 978-0-6488745-0-8 (ebook)
ISBN: 978-0-6488745-1-5 (paperback)

A catalogue record for this book is available from the National Library of Australia

# GLOSSARY

## SPECIES

### Jøran (a.k.a. the kin)
The overarching name for the three species
native to Jørn, which are:

*Qwan (air-kin):* Avians with four eyes and two sets of wings.

*Rucnart (tree-kin):* Gigantic felines with four eyes and six legs.

*Swatai (water-kin):* Small, lizard-like amphibians.

### Jørgen
A Human—Jøran hybrid.

## PSIONICS

### Psion
Someone with the ability to read and/or influence the emotions
and/or thoughts of others (a.k.a. an empath or telepath).

### Aer
A telepathic dream world constructed by the kin.

### Eter
The mental space within an individual's mind, from which they can
construct their own reality and engage with other psions.

### Ora
A mental space accessible only by empaths, where they can
communicate with beings such as Aeotu.

### Anima
The core of a person, also known as their spirit or soul.

## FUG

### Viyu
The technical name for Aeotu's grey-green fug.

### Viyusa
The technical name for red fug.

# IN THE BEGINNING

A lone ship, *Citlali*, wandered through interstellar space. Its crew, a mix of humans and Jørans – intelligent felines and avian with telepathic powers – were tucked up in their cryopods, sleeping away the long journey between solar systems. They trusted *Citlali's* artificial intelligence to guide the way and keep them safe in the great empty void, as they had many times before.

Except this time, the void wasn't empty.

An ancient alien wreck hung in the cold between stars, barely alive and hungry. Very, very hungry. When *Citlali* slowed to investigate, as the AI was programmed to do, the wreck attacked, mould-like nanites attaching themselves to the human ship and eating it. Hull and bulkheads and crew, broken down and ferried through space, materials it would use to repair itself.

By the time Kuma, a Jørgen boy – mostly human but part Jøran too – is woken from stasis/sleep, *Citlali* is dying.

Alone on the malfunctioning ship, Kuma desperately searches for a way to save his friends and family, but especially his twin sister, Grea. It's not until he follows the mould-like nanites back to their source that he discovers a terrifying truth. The alien ship is alive, and it's name is Aeotu.

Lonely and desperate, Aeotu has her own mission. She will swallow *Citlali* whole, and there is nothing Kuma can do about it. Nonetheless, Kuma makes a last-ditch effort to save the crew.

He fails.

# CHAPTER ONE

I don't know how long I've been floating in the stasis unit, talking to the dark. A day? A week? A year? It's hard to tell with the power out and no chronometer to count down the hours. It feels like years. Years of nothing.

I know it's longer than a day because the food ran out long enough ago that I no longer feel my stomach gnawing at my backbone. I've gotten used to it. Used to the gurgle of stomach acids, the growl of gases. At least it's another sound, something other than my own breathing, the hum of silence. Yeah, who knew silence had a sound. I didn't. Not until Core shoved me in the stasis unit and ejected me into space. Alone. Always alone.

I should have crawled into one of the pods, closed the door and drifted off into stasis/sleep. But I didn't. Couldn't.

Mum was out there, and Dad and Grea. *And Dude*, a little part of me whispers, but I shove it back.

Dude's dead. Sucked into vacuum, the liquid in his body boiled away before it froze, hard as rock, cold as space. Or, if the fug got him first, torn apart piece by piece and fed to the alien ship floating out there, hovering over me. Us. Eating *Citlali* to repair itself, tearing apart my home to make itself whole.

Was it my fault? I haven't decided yet.

*Sister.*

The word shivers through the darkness, through my bones, my blood, familiar as my own thoughts. Still, it makes my skin crawl, my insides shrivel, makes me want to cover my ears, curl in a ball and scream. Except the word isn't in my ears, it's deeper than that. It's in my brain. My heart. Crawling around inside me, trying to worm its way into the very core of my being, my anima, the thing that makes me, me.

I can't escape it. It follows me everywhere, a presence in the back of my skull, in the space between the psionic plane and the other place, the one beyond the threads of reality, a dark, endless space where everything is possible.

I should have gone into stasis/sleep, should have slipped into the pod the moment hunger started gnawing at my belly, should have drowned myself in biogel and neurochemicals. Should have left all of this behind. Except I wouldn't have, couldn't have. I know, in the pit of myself that Aeotu would have followed me even there. But maybe, if I'd been in stasis, I could have reached out, connected with the others, with Mum, with Dad. With Grea.

But I didn't. I was too scared. Not of Aeotu, although the alien AI is part of the reason. No, I haven't slept, haven't let myself go into stasis because... Because then I'd know. If they were alive. If they were dead. I don't want to know. If I don't know, I don't have to believe, don't have to think about life without them, without Grea. Don't have to be all alone...

*Sister.*

No.

*Sister.* The voice comes again, shuddering through the air, chilling my skin.

*No.* I say back to it, leaving the thought in my head, letting it echo there.

Silence.

I haven't talked to it before, save to yell at the steelcrete bulkheads, to scream and curse and beg. Not since I slipped into its mind, not since I planted the image of *Citlali* in the deepest part of its being and told it that the ship was home. Not since it woke up. Not since *I* woke it up.

That hasn't stopped it talking to me. Always the same word, always knocking on the back of my skull. And before the emergency power went, leaving me floating here, the air getting colder and colder, it had used the comms.

*Sister.*

*No.*

*SISTER.*

The word is louder this time and there's an insistence to it that hasn't been there before. An urgency.

Aeotu can go to hell.

I curl into a ball.

There's no feeling in my legs, almost none in my hands. With the emergency power gone, there's nothing to keep the atmosphere inside the stasis-unit-turned-escape-pod stable, nothing to recirculate the air, nothing to keep it warm.

The air is getting colder, all the warmth leeching into the vacuum of space. All that's left is the little bit in my body, my heart pumping the blood around. Even the air in my lungs has icicles, I can feel the sting in my throat. I'd probably feel them in my nose, if I could feel my nose.

I really should have gotten in the stasis pod. But what then? I'd die in my sleep? Die *knowing* my parents were dead? My twin? Every soul I'd ever known, gone? I don't want that. I want to remember them alive, want to believe that when Core jettisoned me into space, that somehow, someway, she kept everyone else safe too.

The worry, the memory of that last frantic run through Stasis deck, the holes and cracks in the units around me, the glimpses of other pods with their thin electric shields. It haunts me, sometimes it haunts me enough to get in the pod, to find out what had happened to everyone. But never enough to close the door and power it up.

I don't feel the cold anymore. I don't feel much of anything. I stopped shivering at some point, probably around the same time my eyelids grew heavy, and staying awake took everything I had. No one really tells you that about freezing to death, about how, at some point, it's just like laying down in your bed, soft and warm and all too easy to close your eyes, to drift away.

It's like that now...

...But I don't want to sleep. Sleeping means dreaming, dreaming means nothing to keep me in my head, nothing to keep me from *knowing*.

...Dreams are nice though. I'm huddled up next to Grea, her arms around me, my arms around her, our foreheads pressed together. Sharing breath, sharing thoughts. Sharing *everything*.

'Hey fathead.' She smiles at me.

'Hey poo breath.'

'It took you long enough.'

'I was busy.'

'Doing what? Playing with your hair?'

'It's prettier than yours.'

She scoffs, hugs me tighter. 'No, it's not.'

'Is so.'

Her eyes are dark, darker than the void of nothingness around us. Black, like mine. Wide, the lashes resting against golden cheeks. It's not just the extreme pigmentation that makes her eyes like that, or the way light bounces off the surface of her iris. There's something buried deep in her mind, something she's trying to keep from me. But she can't keep anything from me. We're twins, identical twins, a single living being split in two.

'What?' I ask.

'Nothing.'

I don't say anything, I don't have to. My disbelief floats between us.

She turns away, so my forehead is pressed to the side of hers, the long silky strands of her hair getting messed up in my nose, some of them catching in my mouth.

But she can't escape me, not when we're like this. Just like I can't escape her.

It doesn't take much. Slipping into Grea's mind is as easy as breathing. Easier. She doesn't even try to keep me out.

She can hide shit though, hide it like crazy, and if she really wanted to, if that thing making her eyes dark was really private, she'd have done it. But she hasn't. She wants me to see, to know, even if she can't bring herself to say the words.

She's going to make me pay for it though.

The forefront of her thoughts is a jumble of emotion, all the fear, all the pain rising from the depths of her being formed into a shield around the darkness.

I plunge in.

The pain comes first, a hot white net of lightning rushing over my skin, under it, in it, setting my teeth alight, burning. Burning. Burning. I want to scream, to cry, to let go. The fear comes next, wrapping around the pain, growing off it, *feeding* on it, until one is the other. Paralysing. Endless.

She's making me hurt. She's *making* me hurt. On purpose.

I try to pull away, but suddenly she's everywhere, gripping me tight, her face mashed up against mine, her mind wrapping me in claws of steelcrete. And, Old Terra, it fucking *hurts*.

I gasp. 'Grea, what are you doing?'

Rage hits me in the middle. Grea's rage, tearing at me, reaching back along the path my brain has taken into hers. It stabs me in the heart, splintering into a million tiny pieces, seeking the core of me, the frozen place in my middle. Trying to light it on fire.

'Grea!'

She growls, teeth bared, her arms bands of steelcrete. 'I'm saving you.'

'I don't need you to save me.'

'Yes, you do. You're giving up, Kuma. You're *leaving* me.'

'You're already dead.' The words are out of me before I know it, rushing from the dark, scared place at the pit of my anima.

'No, I'm not. You're just scared I *might* be dead and too chickenshit to actually. Find. Out.' Those last words she punctuates by punching my shoulder, fist driving into the flesh with hard, meaty *THUMPS*.

Pain. Pain and fear ricochet through her, to me. And that thing – curled behind her eyes, wrapped in her emotions – explodes between us.

I want to retch, to dissolve, to be anywhere but here, to know *this*.

'No.' I shake my head, forehead rubbing against hers. 'You didn't. You *couldn't*.'

'You showed her how.'

'No!'

'It's not what you think. *Aeotu's* not what you think.'

'She's trying to eat us!'

'She's trying to survive, and now she's trying to help *us* survive, because of you. You, Kuma.' Grea catches hold of my face, pinning me with her stare. It's not just my sister looking at me out of her dark eyes, it's the other thing too, something big. Older. Alien.

I whisper its name. 'Aeotu.'

It breathes, wrapping around Grea, moulding her. Changing her arms, her hands. It wriggles under her face until there's a second set of eyes beneath Grea's, another mouth, another nose. A whole second face peering from underneath her skin.

*'Sister,'* it says, and reaches for me.

# CHAPTER TWO

I don't wake up. Waking would imply I was asleep, but I wasn't. I know that, deep in my bones. I am simply aware. Aware of the passage of time, not just minutes or hours or days, but years. Aware that I'm not cold, or hungry or... anything really. I just am. Aware too, that I'm no longer in the stasis unit, that at some point in the unknown passage of time since Grea found me, I was moved. Not under my own power, with my own two legs, but that someone or something picked me up and put me here, wherever here is.

And I am not alone; there are other beings with me, minds that brush against mine that seem familiar and strange at the same time. Their names hover on the edge of my tongue but the restless coils of energy I sense don't belong to the faces playing behind my eyes, not entirely. It's the colours permeating them, the kaleidoscope of blues and greens and the colours for which there are no names, that ones I didn't know existed until I met Aeotu.

There used to be more of the others, filling the space with questions, things I wanted to answer but couldn't, but they've faded, disappeared one-by-one. Those that are left don't talk anymore.

Or maybe I simply don't hear them over the heartbeat; the deep, steady *ttthruum* echoing in the space beyond my chest, my being. It is mine and yet it is not, like my lungs.

I breathe and my lungs are... strange. They don't expand or contract but there's a rush in and then out, gases flooding a million tiny filters that make a giant-sized whole. More than that though, I...

*feel* isn't the right word. There's a whole load of new somethings in my head, a universe of sensations all coming to me at once, every one of them different and yet just alike enough that I know they're mine.

I don't have names for them, don't have a way to describe how they slide into my awareness, finding places to dock, pathways through my brain, like microscopic cargo palettes running on newly laid mag-lines.

And still, as strange as all of this is, as weird, it doesn't *feel* strange. It just… is.

It's like how I know I haven't been asleep, how I know this isn't a dream and I'm not in the stasis unit anymore, floating in vacuum as I slowly freeze to death. It's the same way I know it's been a long time since Aeotu took *Citlali*, since I lost Dude, since I talked to Grea.

A *very* long time. The span stretches out behind me, a shadow on my awareness, a sense of things happening but no real memory of them.

Is this how an AI feels when it comes online? Reading the logs, knowing things without conscious memory of them?

Discomfort rolls through my spine, but the need to move is stifled by my own body, a blockage in the nerves, stopping the need to wriggle my toes and flex fingers, from making it to my muscles.

The discomfort builds, growing teeth and gnawing on my bones. I *need* to move. The sensation rolls through my being, the teeth turning to flames, the flames to magma, the molten rock bottled up at the base of my skull, burning through my neurones. My scalp tightens, trying to hold it in.

But why? Why can't I move?

I try to turn over, try to lift my head, my hands, but none of it responds and the pressure grows. I'm going to explode, going to shatter into a million tiny fragments.

I just need to… Move!

Something gives, exploding outward. Fire runs down my spine, through my chest, fills my hands with magma, burns through my legs, pulls a scream from my throat.

The sound echoes.

Echoes and echoes and echoes.

And suddenly I'm free, or almost.

I struggle to open my eyes, to *see*. There's something holding them shut, something sticky plastered over my eyelids, melting over my cheeks and skull, and it's moving.

Wriggling and crawling, tickling my nose, brushing the sides of my mouth. It's not just on my head either. Now that I've recognised it, I can feel it everywhere, coating my body, parts of it pressing into my stomach, wrapping in coils around my legs, holding my arms to my sides.

What's going on? Where am I?

'Grea!' Again, my voice echoes like I'm in some kind of cavern, or the Ag deck – one of the massive sections that seem to go on forever, with rows and rows upon rows of growth walls, my voice bouncing between them.

Grea doesn't answer.

But something does, something that starts as a rumble and builds, inaudible, felt instead of heard. Starting in my toes, shivering in my legs, a hum under my skin. The stuff around me, holding my eyes shut and my muscles in place, rolls with the sound/feeling, pulsing and squirming until it reaches my ears.

It's a hum at first, a tickle in my ear, and slowly it grows until I can *almost* hear something, a faint *sissss*. And I think, I think I know what it is... I strain toward the sound.

'Sissss...ster.'

No.

'Sisster,' it says again and my insides go cold.

I want to shake my head, to pull away, to run, but the sticky moving stuff holds me tight.

'No, go away!'

A breath of air against my cheek, a movement like lips pressing against flesh. 'Sister.'

'No!' I explode.

Not an actual explosion, not blood and flesh and bone shooting out in a wet red mess of meat and tissue, flying outward at two-thousand pounds per square inch, but a psionic one; an explosion of fear.

It rips out of me on a shockwave of bright screaming yellow, sticky and hot. Acidic. Coating everything it touches, burning through its defences, sinking beneath its skin, diving deep into its bones. Inescapable.

The *emote* takes all of my fear, all the pain, the doubt, the loneliness. The moment Dude leapt from my shoulder; Core/drone pushing me into the stasis unit; the hatch sealing, the "DANGER, VACUUM" sign over the emergency release. Grea in her pod, surrounded by fug and darkness. P'Endr dying. Lyn Captain with her hand reaching out of hardened stasis gel. The sour, musty scent of rot and death. The *CRUNCH* of critter skeletons under my elbows.

Everything. The emote takes *everything*.

Somewhere distant, a scream rends the air. High and piercing, a knife in my ears. Inhuman. As I lose consciousness, slip back into the not-sleep, I sense something... familiar, white around a core of boiling black.

*Onah?*

*Kuma?* My name is an explosion of joy and surprise, carried on an image of qwan chicks, bright and fluffy, huddled in a nest. I have the sense that Onah is searching, that he is not alone and that... Sadness, it hovers under the brightness of the other emotions, coats his mind in a layer of blue-black, weighing him down, making his wings heavy and his talons slow. There is something else behind it, another emotion twisting his insides.

Guilt.

Why? It's not his fault I am here, and I want to ask what it is that pulls at his heart, but the darkness drags me under.

*We are coming, little kin.* Onah's voice and the sharp stab of his grief follow me into sleep. *You will be free.*

✦

There is darkness, and when I come back to myself, it's different. The awareness is gone, the sense of my lungs being huge, the discomfort of needing to move.

I'm empty.

There's no fear, no confusion. Nothing.

It all went into the *emote*.

I'm hollow and tired. So tired.

A rustle. The musty scent of feathers. The hot wash and meaty stench of breath on my face.

I'm still blind, but in the eter – the mental space those of us with the ability read minds call home – there is a dance of light and movement; the sharp, restless growl of a rucnart and the chill crystal of a qwan. Emotions spill around them, blue-black waves of grief and fear mixed with the red of anger and the sharp white of determination. I want to reach out, touch them, to yell that I'm here, but I'm wrapped in fatigue, cocooned and… and…

Guilt; duty; sad-pain, the kind that comes not from sliced skin or broken bones, but from the heart. The emotions bombard my brain. Not human or Jørgen, but kin. For a moment, I see myself on the eter, little more than a lump in the darkness, barely recognisable as human, and there is h'Rawd. The tree-kin leader stands over me, his four giant forepaws planted either side of my torso, the wicked talons made for climbing trees kneading the floor, and his long angular muzzle hovering over my throat.

The emotions I feel are *his* and they're directed at *me*.

Why? And where is Onah?

I smell blood – bright, crisp, coppery – washing my face. There's no time to wonder at it, because with the scent comes the sensation of whiskers on my chin, the wet press of a nose, and the cold, sharp points of teeth closing over my jugular.

It short circuits my brain.

Stop! It's me, Kuma! Crew! Get away! But the words are locked within me, my mind sluggish, psionics trapped behind a wall of not-sleep.

There's pain, the warm wash of blood. My blood. I feel it rise out of the pinpricks in my skin, splash around h'Rawd's fangs. Guilt and duty, h'Rawd's emotions are washing around me, rising with my blood and—

Rage. Red. Screaming. It rips across the eter, reminds me of the thing behind Grea's eyes, of the darkness.

Yowls, snarls, the high-pitched wail of an air-kin. H'Rawd's teeth are gone, leaving only the scent of blood behind.

There's movement, the heavy *thud* of metal hitting flesh, the howl of an injured rucnart, and still that rage, flowing over me like fire, bringing with it the scent of cherries and Grea's presence. It goes on forever, until my ears are numb to the sound and rage settles over me, a blanket – comforting.

It ebbs slowly, disappearing into distance and time, until it's gone, taking h'Rawd and Grea with it.

I sleep.

✳

'Kuma?' Grea, whispering in my ear. 'Are you okay?'

I turn, shifting in the dark place like rolling over under a blanket. 'Yes. H'Rawd didn't hurt me.'

'He would have.' Rage blooms around Grea. 'Onah would have let him.'

'Why?'

'They're scared, but don't worry, I'm here.'

'But why? I haven't done anything.'

'You've changed.'

'I have? How?'

There's silence, it stretches on forever and I'm beginning to wonder if Grea's still there, when she speaks. 'I need to see you,' she says.

'I'm here.' And I guess it's true, if I discount the fact that I don't know where *here* is. It feels like the eter but bigger, emptier. It feels like that place between the threads of reality, where I spoke to Aeotu.

'It's the ora,' Grea says.

'The ora?'

'That place, between the threads.' Grea's forehead on mine, her arms wrapping around my shoulders. 'Somewhere just for us.'

*Us* rings with potential, with depth and volume, with more than just my sister and I. *Us* feels like hundreds of twins, thousands, millions, feels like an entire species and the idea of it is too big, too *much* as it tries to force its way into my head.

I thrust it away. 'I don't understand.'

Grea smiles. I don't see it, *can't* see it, not in this alien, lightless place, but it settles in my chest. Warm. Comforting. Secure. 'It's okay,' Grea says. 'You will soon.' Her arms tighten. 'I'll help you.'

I find my arms, hug her back. 'Okay.'

'Just you wait.' Grea turns her head, and while she's with me in the ora, her thoughts are with someone— some*thing* else. 'We're going to live forever.'

This time when I wake, I know I've been dreaming, know that the thing that had me was sleep.

I open my eyes.

Darkness still assails me, but my lids move. And when I lift my hand to check for the sticky stuff that held them down, it obeys my command, the fingers flexing and curling, dragging over my face. There's something hard covering my head, a rough second skin. It crumbles under my touch, and I come away with some kind of powdery substance. I wipe it away from eyes, use my other hand and peel sections of it from my hair. The stuff cracks, and then as soon as I pull it away it crumbles, slipping through my fingers, smooth and silky.

I still can't see and I rub at my face, digging fingers into my eyes, feeling smooth warm skin, the soft, spiky brush of eyelashes, the bump of my nose. There's nothing there but dermis, nothing holding my eyelids, and yet sight eludes me.

I rub harder, searching in the corners for the crust of sleep. Try again.

Success.

The darkness is no longer the total nothingness of the void. There's enough light to see the smudge of my fingers. I don't know where it's coming from, it seems to be everywhere.

I can't even see my feet. But I can move them.

Standing is strange. The ingrained movement of muscle is there – pulling my feet under me, shifting my weight – but the details... It's like I'm wearing flippers and there are weights on my knees, like maybe there's a sack of machine parts on my back throwing me out of whack. Making me top-heavy and knock-kneed.

Have I grown?

But that's not right either, doesn't *feel* right. Not in the sense that my body feels different, 'cause it does, but in the sense that it doesn't gel with the *awareness* that came before.

I've been out for a long time, long enough, awareness tells me, to grow enough that I no longer look like the Kuma I once did. But that's not it. I think, if I could find a mirror, or a holo or even just a light, that I would still *look* like me. A kid with black hair and a lanky frame, kinda skinny and maybe a little rounder in the hips than other boys, but still... a kid.

It's something else, and that awareness is holding onto the answer, hoarding it deep in my gut. And I want to know why and I want to know what. I want to get rid of this awful, horrible sense building in the pit of my anima, that when I find out... When I find out, the psionic explosion of before is going to look like a fart in the ocean.

But first...

The ground's uneven, and trying to walk with my too-long feet and too-heavy torso is hard. I stumble, stagger, fall to my knees. Not being able to see makes it harder, not knowing where I am makes it worse, and the memory of Aeotu whispering against my cheek, the feel of her breath...

How does an AI breathe? How does its voice ripple up my legs and vibrate in my ear?

My heart's pounding, and like when I first became aware, it feels weird. My heart is too big, cavernous, flooding my veins not with blood but power.

*THUMP. THUMP. THUMP.*

'Sister.'

I jerk back into myself, into my weird, top-heavy body still feeling my cavernous lungs and massive heart, and somehow knowing they're not mine. Not my flesh. Not my blood.

The voice comes again, rippling through the gloom, rushing over the uneven ground and up my legs. 'Sister.'

I spin, pinwheeling my arms to keep my feet. 'Go away,' I yell. And just about jerk out of my skin at the alien sound that erupts from my chest.

The words are mine, but the voice isn't.

Too deep, too loud. Too... metallic.

For a second, I wonder if my voice has dropped or if someone slipped testosterone into my system during the time I wasn't aware.

But no, that doesn't make sense, doesn't feel right. Doesn't even sound right. There's something wrong with me.

The awareness in my gut doesn't agree.

Okay. Okay.

Don't panic.

Yeah, Kuma. Don't panic. You're just in a big dark place, with a weird body, ship-sized lungs and an alien entity creeping up behind you. No need to panic. You're fine.

Now.

Run.

There's strength in these weird legs of mine, a new bound in my too-long feet, and the lungs that are drawing in so much air, I don't think I'll ever have to breathe again.

It's riding on the speedway, palette going so fast it presses your ribs into your heart and flattens your face. Except on the speedway, I can see.

Three strides and I'm flat on my face, the same soft powdery shit I wiped off it gumming up my tastebuds, gluing my tongue to the roof of my mouth, clogging up my nose.

It tastes like mould, dry and dusty, and it *tingles*.

There's no time to scrape it off, no moisture to spit it out, there's just the thing coming up behind me, rustling over the uneven ground, reaching for my ankle.

I'm on my feet, running.

There's light ahead, a bright spot in the gloom. Safety. Every pound of my feet raises a puff of powder, every unexpected dip in the ground catches my feet, tips my body, makes me fight to stay upright. Panic and fear and adrenalin, they're rushing through my veins.

Making my muscles push harder, my vision sharper. The bright spot ahead is a hatch. Rounded and smooth with *Citlali's* six-pointed star in the middle.

Relief. Hope. They pound through my chest, and from somewhere I find another spurt of strength to push myself forward.

Behind, the rush of the voice is getting closer, nipping at my heels. It doesn't speak, it doesn't have to.

I just need to get to the hatch, to reach *Citlali*.

I'll be home then. Safe.

The light is all around me and the hatch is there, under my hands, and I'm pushing against it, and it's sliding open and then I'm beyond and the door is closing. I get a glimpse of the space behind it, of the grey darkness, the powder, and Aeotu, rushing along in my wake. Except there's nothing there. No shape, no shadow, just the endless grey-black.

The hatch snaps shut.

I stare at it. Take in the smooth, flat steelcrete, a little pock-marked, scratches marring the surface, ragged marks like claws cutting deep into the steelcrete.

And the symbol, *Citlali's* star, glowing over it, bright as the sun.

Around me are the familiar off-white corridors, the hush of air-cyclers and the sharp lines of the deck plating, all looking like the fug never touched it.

I sag, bones turning to mush, adrenalin turning to exhaustion, panic and fear to relief. Home. I'm home.

And then I look down.

# CHAPTER THREE

Oh shit.

I stumble, my knees, my weird, too-big knees, turning to jelly.

Oh shit.

I knew, knew deep inside that things were different. Were weird, were not what they should be but...

Oh shit. Ohshitohshitohshitohshit.

I back-peddle, but it's like I'm trying to walk away from myself. Wobble. Wobble. Half-run. *WHOMP*. My back hits the bulkhead, and there's nowhere else to go, nothing to do but lift my arms out to my sides and stare at the... the...

Are they feet? They kind of look like feet, kind of look like paws too. Really big, grey-green paws, with three stubby toes like an Old Terran emu and darker, almost black nubs that might be claws... My toes flex almost of their own accord and... Wow. Those aren't claws, those are big fucking knives on the end of my feet, as long as my hand, as thick as two fingers combined and...

*Skrrriiiitch.*

My toes curl and I can't help but flinch at the sharp screech, like fingernails on blackboard, except it's my new toenails on steelcrete, leaving gouges in the decking deep enough to make a rucnart jealous. Or afraid. Very, very afraid.

Like me, right now.

But the shit doesn't stop there.

My new, paw-feet are fuzzy, and not from fur, although I guess you could call it fur, except fur doesn't move, doesn't *wriggle* all on its own. I swallow, hard, because I know what that shit is, know it because I burnt it, pointed the Franken-thrower at it and watched it shrivel up and die. Heard it scream.

Fug. My feet are coved in fug.

I'm hyperventilating, breath coming short and fast, coming like it's never going to come again, and in that distant part of me, I feel those huge cavernous lungs wheezing, see lights going off, feel... things running across big struts that make up its ribs and—

As if having fug-feet wasn't bad enough, the nano-tech, ship-eating mould is covering my shins, crawling over my shipsuit, climbing all the way up my thighs until it hugs my hips, and—

I don't want to look at my hands, really I don't, but they're just kind of there, in front of my face and... There's fug on them as well, wrapping around my fingers, trailing over the back of my hands, looping around my wrists and winding up my forearms. It stops at the elbow, looking like a critter-nibbled glove over my shipsuit, all lacy and delicate. But green, a sickly, muted, oh-my-god-I'm-gonna-throw-up green.

Vomit spews over the deck, rushes into the grooves my paw-feet dug in the steelcrete before creeping toward my fug-toes.

I'm covered in fug.

I'm covered. In. Fug.

Oh shit.

Panic explodes in my chest, making my heart pound, every muscle shake, and suddenly I'm half crouched and talons have sprouted from my fingers and I'm tearing at my feet. Ripping. Screaming.

I have to get it off. Off. Off. Off.

Every slash of my claws brings pain, horrible slashing pain, pain that goes all the way down to the bone. But it's distant, muffled, like it belongs to someone else.

That just makes me braver, more determined. Brings back a little of my sanity. Fug flies, torn from my feet and flung across the corridor, a hail of grey-green. Every swipe of my fug claws rips another chunk off, more and more and more, a talon, a toe, the top of my foot.

There's no blood. That thought pops up amidst the madness. No oozing, no gushing. No screaming. The fug doesn't fight back like it did with the Franken, doesn't form spikes, doesn't attack my hands. Doesn't do anything.

I tear another chunk off, and there's another colour in the grey-green, a pale gold, flushed rose with blood. Flesh. Kuma flesh.

*Me*. Not fug. *Me*.

Everything in me stops, and for one crystal moment, I feel relief, I feel hope. I feel like this whole freaky, scary, horrible shit-mess is maybe, *maybe* going to turn out all right. Because I'm still me. I'm still *here* under the fug.

It's just a second.

Then that golden patch of skin starts to disappear.

'What? No. No. Nononononono!'

I'm ripping and tearing, digging. But it's not enough. The fug is growing back, filling in the hole, seeping into the rents, pulling itself back together. Faster, faster, faster.

I can't keep up with it. Flesh-me disappears, is gone, and no matter how fast I move, how deep my fug-claws go, the fug grows faster. And not just faster, it's making itself harder.

My fug-claws aren't digging as deep, the furrows they make shallower until they're not making any marks at all, just *screeching* over a new, hard outer shell. As I watch, the shell forms plates, thick and glossy, linked together like the chest plates of a sterdane.

I'm slowing, sweat dripping down my back, panic still boiling in my gut, the worst of it burned out, expended on the manic destruction of my feet, and now buried under a new emotion.

I slump against the bulkhead, unable to take my eyes from the fug-feet. Idly watching as the bits I've torn off, the chunks and strips, crawl back together.

Despair rises up and over my shoulders, turns my brain numb, turns everything numb.

I just...
There's nothing.

Eventually, I get up.

There's no time, but that awareness in the pit of me says it wasn't long. A few minutes at most.

It felt like an hour. An hour in which my brain ceased to function and I stared at my feet, at my hands, at the fug encasing my legs.

I was fug.

I. Was. Fug.

That thought chased itself around my head, one loop and then another and another until I forgot the panic, forgot the despair, and just… was.

Fug.

There's a weird space behind the word, a calm that goes beyond the deep breaths and counting heartbeats. It's a feeling deeper than bone, a sensation that goes all the way to my anima and spreads through my veins. The fug's not eating me, not attacking, not even when I attack it. Of course, I haven't tried burning it yet, but there's nothing around here to burn fug.

The corridor is empty, just the hatch and *Citlali's* symbol glowing away.

*Citlali.*

Of course. The AI will know what to do.

'Core?' My call bounces out of me, the too-deep voice taking me aback, but after discovering my fug-feet, it doesn't worry me like it did.

The AI doesn't answer, but there's a tug at the awareness in my gut telling me to pay attention.

I don't.

'Core?' I try again, louder this time, using those too-big lungs for something other than freaking me out. 'Core!'

Nothing, not even an echo.

Okay. That's weird.

*Citlali's* corridors echo. Sound bounces off the hard walls like rabid bats, around the rings and through the spokes connecting them, fracturing a million times until it comes back at you. But there's nothing, just the *hush* of the air cyclers.

The bulkheads ate my voice. Granted, it's a strange voice, and maybe Core didn't recognise it, what with its deep metallic sound and all, but still... Maybe she's offline. Maybe the fug got her. Maybe, maybe, maybe.

That's when I get to my feet, pushing myself off the wall, wobbling a bit on the fug-paws, trying not to look at them, or at my hands.

I press the spot inside my elbow, the little raised disc where my biocomp implant is. A holo spits and fuzzes over my palm, one of the few bits of clear Kuma skin left. It takes a few seconds for the screen to steady, for me to make out the absolute lack of anything helpful on the blue square of light. Of anything at all.

The screen above my hand is blank, without even Citlali's six-pointed star pulsing over my palm. Okay, don't panic. Just... you're fug, it's probably messing with the biocomp

I just need to reset it. It'll be good once I reset it. I just have to find a maintenance hatch or an engineering section. Yeah, that's all I have to do.

The awareness doesn't agree, tells me I'm dreaming, that I'm ignoring things I shouldn't, that I'm not paying attention.

I start off down the corridor.

I'm okay with ignoring stuff.

I don't know this corridor. It looks like Citlali, with the same boxy hallways, the same curve that bends just enough that you know you're close to the centre of the ship, but it's not Citlali. There are no hatches, no control pads, nothing but the smooth off-white bulkheads and the darker decking. And no matter how often I call, neither Core nor any of her sub-AIs answer.

I've been walking for ages with no sign of another living soul. No sign of fug either, unless you count the Kuma-fug. I've discovered it's not so bad having paw-feet, that the talons on the tips of my fingers make reaching the itchy bit between my shoulder blades a breeze.

It's pretty neat. I could get used to it if it weren't fug.

Fatigue drags at my bones, makes it harder to coordinate my feet. At some point in my interminable march, I found a rhythm, an extra bounce that prevented my claws from leaving divots in the deck. But the rhythm disappeared somewhere in the last half hour, smothered under the weight pulling at my eyelids, making my head droop.

I can't sleep though; I have to get out of here. Have to find Core.

Something skitters behind me.

Energy pumps through my system.

I spin, no longer uncoordinated, no longer drooping. Talons out, the fug... spreading over the back of my hands, rushing up over my knuckles, forming spiky ridges even as it covers my elbows, filling in the gaps. In the space between heartbeats, I'm no longer wearing lacy fug-gloves, my arms are sheathed in armour.

There's nothing behind me. The corridor is empty, not so much as a shadow disturbing the walls. And still... The awareness says something is wrong, that my eyes aren't seeing what's really there, that I'm not *understanding*.

What's to understand? I'm on a not-*Citlali* chasing my fug-laden arse around a hallway with no end and no doors. Not so much as an intersecting corridor to cut up the monotony of off-white walls.

I can hear the hush of the cyclers moving air, the soft pad of my fug-paws, the gentle *nick nick nick* of my talons, and there's something following me, something I can't see.

The skitter comes again, further away this time.

I follow it.

*Nick, nick, nick.*

*Skitter.*

*Nick, nick, nick.*

Movement, a quiver of light.

Pause. Tension rides through my blood. Not the tension of fear, but of anticipation, of... of... It's familiar but I don't have a name for it.

Awareness whispers at the back of my mind, cold and focussed, full of numbers and facts. *The Hunt.*

Yes. The Hunt. I'm hunting, like the rucnarts. Like the qwans.

Every fibre of my being focuses on the shimmer just a few metres ahead. Not a shadow, but not a light either. A something that doesn't belong, that's trying to hide.

You can't hide from me, little shadow.

I pounce.

The fug-feet take me over the deck separating us in a single leap. For a split-second I'm flying and it's brilliant, and then I'm on the deck, hand-claws snatching at nothing.

There's a squeal and the not-shadow is off, a distortion of light shooting down the corridor. The hunting tension takes over even as my brain tries to pause, tries to catalogue the familiar taste of fuzz on my tongue. I'm bounding after it, a step behind the not-shadow, a centimetre, a nano-metre. Reach down.

It darts sideways.

I snatch at it.

It zags the other way.

Zig. Zag. Snatch. Growl.

That last one is me. Frustration riding up through my throat. There's an idea knocking on the back of my brain, a heavy insistent sound, but the Hunt is all about focus, and right now I'm focused on the not-shadow. On the geometry of its zig and zag, on angles and velocity and the composition of its skin, the chemicals that let it bend light. We'll have to open it up, dig our claws into its belly and rip—

Right. No.

I skid to a stop.

What the fuck was that?

*Ripping* into its *belly*?

*Ewww. Gross.* The thought pops into my brain, and it's not mine.

'Grea?'

*Finished chasing critters?*

'Critters?'

*The not-shadow.* A pause as the voice in my head, the one that sounds like me but with the bright cherry of my twin's mind, focuses elsewhere. Ahead, the not-shadow quivers, the light around it shattering, revealing a golden ball of fuzz. *I asked him to find you. Didn't think he'd do the light-bending thing, but then I guess your new look scared him.*

I hear 'light-bending' and try to figure out when critters got the ability to make themselves invisible, even as Grea's mention of my new look pings on the back of my brain as strange, but my attention is on the critter. On the little black nose and the way he sits, not quite quivering but close enough, and I'm trying to convince myself that he's real, that I'm not imaging things, because the little gold critter I know is dead, got sucked into vacuum and—

'Dude?'

He chitters. Hops forward a few steps.

I'm on my knees. 'Is that you?'

He squeaks.

There's wetness on my cheeks, dripping off my chin.

And then the fug's retreating from my palms and Dude's in my hands, his golden hum vibrating through my skin and settling in my brain. And instead of ripping and tearing, I'm cradling the fuzz-butt under my chin, hand claws fading to nothing, fug receding until my palms are Kuma-flesh.

*All right, it's touching, it really is, but I need you to get off your butt and come get me.*

I close my eyes, still holding Dude close to my chest, and reach back along the sense of my sister, slipping into the eter. The psionic plane is empty, just me and Dude in the endless white.

The little guy is a comforting fuzz on my shoulder, even as

confusion rises in a muddy grey cloud around my feet. I turn, stretching my senses, searching for a trace of Grea, but even though I taste her on the back of my tongue I can't find her. She's everywhere and nowhere at once.

'Where are you?' My voice echoes.

*I don't know.* Loneliness, stark white with a sharp thread of fear vibrates the eter, coming from all around.

'I can't see you.'

*Just find me.*

'How? I don't...' I lift my hands in frustration, letting them slap back against my sides. 'You're coming from *everywhere*, there's no direction.'

*How am I supposed to know? You're the one who's awake.*

I freeze, shock holding me in place. 'You're still in stasis?'

*I—* Anger and frustration flood her presence, and something else, something that crawls down my spine and lodges in my gut, something that makes the *awareness* shiver.

Whatever it is, it isn't right, isn't good.

Dude hums against my cheek.

The *awareness* is gone a moment later, cut off like it never was, taking Grea with it.

'Grea!' I zip around the eter. 'Grea!'

I can't lose Grea, not after I just found her—

*I'm here, fathead.* She speaks from behind me.

I spin around, and there she is, a shimmer on the psionic plane.

'Where'd you go? What's going on?'

*I already told you.* Anger crosses her face, lights up the space around her with brilliant sparks of red. *I don't know.*

I'd believe her too, except there're whispers of black in the halo around her hands and threading through her hair. Lies.

'You're lying.'

The red glows brighter, even as her hands clench into fists. *I'm not.*

'I can see it, Grea. You know I can.'

Her mouth contorts, twisting, and then she's in my face, nose-to-nose. *Just find me, little brother.*

'Why are you lying?'

A fist thumps into my chest, pushing me back with enough force to send me flying. I slam to the ground, the impact driving the wind from my lungs, leaving me gaping at my twin. Her nose still pressed to mine, her brows dark slashes over void-dark eyes, and that *thing*, that *something* swimming in their depths.

The awareness in my gut whispers, "Euvia" and there is danger on its breath.

*Find me,* Grea says one last time, and then she's gone.

# CHAPTER FOUR

Find me.

I'm back in the *Citlali* corridor that isn't, staring at the same bulkhead, Dude perched on my shoulder.

Find me, she says, like she's the ultimate authority on what I should do. Like she knows better.

Typical Grea.

Maybe she does. That thing behind her eyes worries me, the lies wrapping around her, and that little voice of awareness whispering 'Euvia'.

The name stirs a memory of escape and loneliness, of leaving a half of me behind. It makes my heart ache with a pain that isn't mine, but I can't put a face to it, can't recall *how* I know her. Who is Euvia and why does she make me think of fire and screaming? Why am I afraid?

The fear does not match the memory of loneliness, of being split in two, it's deeper than that, buried in a maze of confusion and dread, wrapped up in sticky strands of darkness. It takes me awhile to dig it out but when I do, it's obvious the emotion isn't mine, that it's old, ancient even, and that brings with it a whole new set of questions. Who does it belong to? How'd they stick it in *my* head?

There's no answer, not even a niggle from the awareness in my gut, not even when I delve back into the etre and pry it apart. Nothing except a curious shimmer, like if I twisted my brain a little, I might see something new.

That reminds me of Aeotu, and Aeotu brings me back to the physical, to the fug cocooning my body.

I don't want to think about the alien ship, and yet... I flex the fug feet. There's no real way I *can't* think about it.

Dude hums and the sound soothes my nerves, spreading gold through my mind.

I flex my feet again, first one toe and then the other, the thick black-green talons popping out of the tips, scraping against the steelcrete, right next to another, deeper furrow, one with the dried remnants of vomit crusted in the bottom.

Yeah.

I take a deep breath. In through the nose, out through the mouth, and stare at the furrows.

Yeah.

If I *had* been thinking about Aeotu, about how *Citlali's* symbol just appeared, about all the things that happened before Core shoved me into that stasis unit... Disgust twists my insides. If I'd been thinking about all of those things instead of rushing around in circles, trying to find a way out of the endless corridor, freaking out over the fug-feet, if I'd listened to the awareness in my gut, I might have twigged a little sooner. Might have found Grea by now.

I'm on the alien ship. On Aeotu, and whatever it's done to me, it's probably done to *Citlali*.

To Mum, to Dad. And what about Grea? What has it done to her, what is she hiding from me?

Was *this* happening to her right now? Was she in the darkness somewhere, held down while Aeotu gave her fug-feet? Who else? Who else is still alive? Who else has fug-feet and fug-hands, who else hears that sibilant 'sister' shivering through the air? Who else is totally and utterly freaked out?

Who's going to save *me*?

Dude presses a tiny paw to my cheek, and I know, as if he's saying it, that *he's* saving me, and now I gotta go save Grea, because that's what little brothers do.

I heave out a breath, directing it upwards so it flips the fringe dangling in my eyes. 'Yeah. Yeah, I know Dude, it's all on me.'

He pats my cheek.

✳

The bulkhead SNAPS downwards, dumping me in a corridor as unlike the last as my fleshy self is to the fug-paws. It's not just the shape of the corridor, like an oval turned on its side, or the patterns etched in the curving bulkheads. It's the chaos.

A battlefield.

An *alien* battlefield.

These are not *Citlali's* corridors, not by a long shot; walls flow into ceilings and floors, no corners, no sharp lines except for the carvings. Intricate patterns cover every millimetre of the bulkheads, not just drawing the eye but sucking it in and holding it captive. It takes effort not to look, especially when the patterns appear to move, twisting and turning, like shadows melting one into the other.

Something in the pit of me, that *awareness*, whispers that the carvings have meaning, that I should pay attention, but I've been down that rabbit hole before and I'm not getting caught again. Especially not when scorch marks stain the pale grey walls, claw marks are gouged deep into the intricate carvings, and the deck is thick with ragged clumps of fug and the desiccated bodies of critters.

I crouch beside one clump, suddenly glad of the fug covering my hands as I dig through a pile of grey-green dust to uncover one of the little bodies. It's mostly skeleton with a few ragged bits of muscle and tendon strung between the bones. On my shoulder, Dude is silent for a moment, tension riding his body before he scurries down my arm and perches on the back on my hand, his gaze intent on the corpse.

I'm not sure if critters mourn the way we do. They have such short lives – scurrying around doing our dirty work – that I kind of wonder if they acknowledge death at all. A little part of me, deep in the back of my mind, wonders how long I'll have Dude. I've already lost him once. I don't want to do it again.

Dude is still studying the dead critter, tension clenching his muscles, but now he's reaching out to it, five sets of tiny claws sinking into the back of my hand as he stretches the sixth toward the corpse. He's barely touched it before he's shooting back up my arm, fur all sleeked out and his little muzzle pulled back in a snarl worthy of a rucnart.

'Dude?'

*Wrongness* emanates from the little guy, a muddy yellow that skitters up the back of my neck and has me snatching my hand back from the corpse, standing fast enough to give myself the spins.

I stare at the skeleton, fascination and dread gluing my gaze to it the same way spilled intestines might. It looks just like any other critter, not that I've seen many dead ones, but that *wrongness*... I shiver and back away, surveying the carnage with new eyes, attention catching anew on the furrows in the walls, the scorch marks next to them.

My heart leaps at the evidence of *Citlali's* crew, of kin claws and human flame-throwers, but questions crowd out the joy.

How long *was* I in the place where Onah and h'Rawd found me? But most important, when did the crew wake up and second... What *happened* here? To the critters, to the walls, to the fug? Were the crew fighting the critters? Were the critters fighting the fug? Were they all fighting each other?

Most of the fug is dead or dying, the vines dull and grey, some crumbled to dust, others patchy and torn, like critters have been chewing on them. Or fug. Grey-green dominates what's left of the nanite jungle, but there are splashes of red amongst the carnage, blooms of the same fug I saw in those last few moments before Core shoved me into the stasis unit. They tug at my memory, trying to pull something from the depths of my time in the darkness, flooding me with memories of hot breath and sharp teeth, of a tsunami of rage crashing through the psionic plane. Of Grea.

My heart's thumping, *BANG BANG BANG* against my ribs, squeezing out the air.

I don't want to remember. I don't want to—

Dude, his paw against my cheek, pushing the memories and the panic aside.

My heart slows and I breathe – in through the nose, out through the mouth. 'Thanks, Dude.'

He chitters and pats my chin.

I should probably be concerned about those memories, about what they mean, and I am – really, I am – but now's not the time for a panic attack. Not the time to contemplate why a rucnart would have their teeth at my throat.

At least the kin are alive, or were alive. At some point. How long was I out? I drag a hand over a bulkhead, fingers tracing the claw marks, hesitating over the red-brown splash of what looks like blood.

I have to find the crew.

Glows light the corridor, red and yellow and orange, where there's light at all, flashing and spitting. Most of it is dark, shadows piled atop shadows.

The fug-feet make no sound as I... pad, I guess I pad now. I guess I can even say I stalk, although that makes me think of h'Rawd and *he* makes me think of the claws that raked across Aeotu's walls, and *that* summons other memories, training memories, of ancient rucnarts stalking underground hallways that looked just like this one. Brings back the taste of *Them*, of white throats in my jaws, the musty taste of their blood, their screams as the water-kin crushed their minds.

Yeah. Stalking sounds cool until you remember that. So, not stalking, but still, the fug-feet don't just *walk*, there's a springiness in the ankle, a bounce that turns my regular human stride into something more, into something *other*.

Glide, let's go with glide.

I *glide* down the corridor, moving around crumbled sections of bulkheads and mounds of dull grey fug. Stepping nimbly over the remains of critters. And all of it happens without thinking, without me even really noticing. Those other senses, the ones I felt when I first became *aware*, play in the back of my mind, telling me things like the oxygen-nitrogen ratio and the rate of decay of the bodies on the deck. They tell me other things too, things that have no place, that spin in my brain looking for a home, some of them find meaning in parts of me that don't *feel* like me, like the fug-feet. And even though I can't understand it, I can sense the communication between them, and that... that doesn't disturb me like it should.

Not like the dark mountain of fur ahead.

I stop. Not just stop but *freeze*, every hair, every muscle, every fug-laden part of me still as the shadows around us.

I can't make out much in the dark, can't see more than the lumpy silhouette with its fuzzy outline, but an alarm is ringing in my head, a new surge of adrenalin dumped into my bloodstream. Fear colours the tension, brings with it the memory of hot breath and teeth, makes my shoulders hunch and my stomach knot, but it's all buried beneath the sudden painful focus of the Hunt.

The mountain doesn't move. It's sprawled across the corridor, the red and orange of flickering glows picking out bits of fur, highlighting the sharp points of ears and muscled limbs.

That awareness tells me it's not fug. For a moment, I wonder if it's one of *Them*, if somehow one of the aliens stayed behind when Aeotu was evacuated, somehow survived half a millennium floating in the depths of interstellar space on a ship slowly cannibalising itself.

But the awareness says no, tells me a story of biology too low in fat stores, of claws that are designed to climb trees and jaws to tear flesh from bones. Tells me too that the mountain breathes, that its heart beats faster since I opened the hatch. That it's waiting for me.

There's only one thing that climbs trees on the *Citlali*. A tree-kin.

In the back of my brain, the Hunt tenses, a warning that feels old, ancient like the sticky strands of darkness from before, ringing.

I push it aside.

'Hello?' The too-deep voice booms from my chest, and is swallowed by the bulkheads.

The mountain twitches, irritation blooming in the air around it. Relief blooms in my chest, which you might think is strange, but kin – tree-kin especially – aren't fans of verbal communication, and now I know it's not fug I'm talking to.

'Hey,' I say again. 'I know you're awake. I'm Kuma, I'm crew.'

I take a stiff, halting step forward. The fug-feet are fighting me, the Hunt is fighting me, wants me to stay put, to shut up and wait the other hunter out. But I can't, and they're *my* feet, Old Terra damn it, the fug's just hijacking them.

The mountain doesn't move but I sense the tension coming off it, a red-veined ripple in the air. The red smells of bloodlust and rage, and the Hunt rises, grips my insides and demands I halt.

I fight it, taking another shuddering step forward.

'Do you need help?' I say again.

A snarl. Bloodthirsty.

The rucnart rises. Slowly, one inch at a time. Shoulders first, then haunches, almost as if she's stretching. The last thing to rise is her head, swinging around, pinning me with all four eyes.

H'Lott. Tall and lean with a stumpy tail, her coat a hundred shades of orange-gold, perfect for blending into the harsh sands of Jørn's largest desert. She's a sub-matriarch, just below p'Ender in the clan. Only h'Rawd outranks her. Only h'Rawd is scarier.

She's never much liked those of us on two legs, always going out of her way to avoid us. I've only met her a few times, enough to know she reserves a special hatred for Grea and me. I'd once wondered if we'd done something, stepped on her paws or snatched her favourite protein slab, or if her hate was something we represented, an old memory she couldn't shake. Or maybe her dislike stemmed from years spent on a ship with humans. I guess now isn't the time to ask.

Menace drips from the gleam of her fangs, pushes outward from her eyes.

For a moment, a split-second, I remember my time in the dark, remember the scrape of teeth, the prickle of whiskers over my chin. It's just a moment, just a wobble, but it's all the Hunt needs to take me over.

One moment I'm all me with just this little bit of *other* talking in the back of my brain, and then I'm not. Or, kind of me but *other* too.

And that part, that *other*... Hate is the wrong emotion to describe what it feels, because it doesn't feel, doesn't *hate* like I know it, doesn't experience that volcano of emotion erupting from its core. What it experiences, both better and worse, is the drive not to destroy but annihilate, to leave nothing of h'Lott behind but blood and memory.

It rises through my bones, turning my muscles to steelcrete. Me, Kuma, the boy who loves critters and cried over a carpet of the dead fuzzbutts, who tried to save a dying rucnart. That boy is pushed aside. Buried. Encased in metal and left to pound against the walls of his cage.

I'm the Hunt now, and I remember fleeing before a wave of teeth and terror, of creatures that rose out of the ground and tore my creators apart with teeth and claws. Of others, unseen, who reached into the sister-brain and turned us into killers, made the creators sabotage and then abandon us.

I remember them.

I'm still here, still watching h'Lott snarl in the darkness, fear blooming in my gut, but the *emote* I should be summoning, should be rolling toward her on an inescapable wave of calm... it's stuck behind the anger surfing through my amygdala, triggering fight or flight hormones and turning my blood to ice.

*Come and get it,* that part of me says, the part that's Hunt, that feels nothing, no guilt, no remorse, and leaves nothing of its enemies behind.

The real me, the bit that's peering through the mask of the other, that bit flinches, wants to throw up.

H'Lott's snarl falters.

Opportunity. Hunt urges me forward.

The fug-feet glide, smooth, silent save for the *NICK NICK* of the claws.

She backs up. One step, two, every movement in sync with mine.

*{{ Danger. }}* The awareness flashes the word in my mind, presses on me the perception of another heat signature, another vibration in the decking.

But that bit of me that is Hunt is tangled up in the human me and it doesn't care. H'Lott is mine, this corridor is mine. Her flesh will tear beneath my claws, her teeth will crack on the armour growing over my shoulders and neck, and she will scream in that high, piercing death-yowl and—

A shadow, seen too late.

The awareness screams. *{{ Danger! }}*

I spin. H'Rawd leaping out of darkness, fangs and claws and the mad, mad blaze of his eyes.

No time to brace, only time to hang on, to dig fug-claws into fur as almost nine-hundred kilos of fury hits me in the chest.

What little bit of Kuma that was left is gone, there's just Hunt now, just the *TH-THUMP* of my heart, the rush of adrenalin, the cold hard embrace of the fug encasing my arms, my legs, my chest. The awareness pumps data into my brain, tells me about the vulnerable spot just behind the rucnart's skull. And now I'm twisting and turning, clinging to h'Rawd's neck, climbing onto his back, and the hand-claws are no longer claws, but blades, matt-green and curved, springing from the backs of my hands. I lift one over my head, that vulnerable spot clear in my mind's eye—

A roar. A weight slamming into my side.

The deck. The constellation of Kuma going off in front of my eyes. The cage around the real me cracks, and for a moment I am Kuma, just Kuma and then rage blasts through me. H'Lott's and h'Rawd's rage. All of it hitting me in the chest, blending one into the other until there's no telling which emotion belongs to whom, or if they're mine.

They *are* all mine. Once I feel them, I know them, they belong to me, they *answer* to me, roll over and play dead for me. Never piss off an empath, that's all I'm going to say, especially not one rocking a new internal *other*.

I gather the emotion into a ball, draw it into my chest and whisper to it, listen to its secrets, the loose threads of thought and memory it drags from its hosts. Images of betrayal, memories of death, flashes of grief, the need to protect and avenge. I grow it, nurture it, turn it around and tell it a different story, one of fear, one of defeat. And then I throw it back.

H'Lott collapses, her weight pinning my legs to the deck, while h'Rawd freezes, his eyes, all four of them, wide, his head up and throat exposed.

Victory pumps through my veins, gives me the strength to rise, to grab a dying fug-vine, to pump energy into it, to draw it back and—

My muscles seize, holding me fast.

Gold sinks through my brain, pushing back the rage, fracturing the walls of the cage that keep Kuma contained.

I'm me again. Hunt is gone, and with it my energy. The fug-vine crumbles to dust and my back hits the deck. Exhaustion is dragging at my bones, hunger clawing at my belly, but at least it's not h'Lott's teeth. Not yet at least.

H'Rawd shakes, a violent full-body movement like he's trying to dislodge old biogel from his fur. In a way he is, but an emote is harder to get rid of than that, calls on things buried deep within and sticks to them, an industrial-grade psionic nano-glue.

Another reason the kin don't like empaths. Although they always seemed to get along with Grea well enough, so it's probably just me.

Determination and anger radiate from h'Rawd, pulsing outward, but the defeat and that sinking, sickening fear still has him tight in its grip.

'I'm crew.' My voice is scratchy, hoarse.

He snarls, legs shaking as he stalks closer.

I hold up a hand, not entirely sure what I'm going to do, how I'm going to stop an angry tree-kin with my legs pinned. 'I'm—'

"Crew" gets stuck on my lips as Dude rushes up my arm and leaps right at h'Rawd's bared fangs.

I don't know how he does it, but somehow, instead of becoming critter bait, Dude is sitting on the tree-kin's snout, clinging to the bridge of his nose and staring him in the eye. Not the lower ones, mind, but the upper ones, that ones the kin open just before they turn you into a psionic shish-kabob.

And Old Holy Terra, h'Rawd doesn't eat him.

In fact... Are h'Rawd's ears rising? Is his muzzle un-wrinkling?

I think my jaw is on the floor, mouth open wide enough for Dude to hop in there.

What is the little guy doing?

The eter is a thought away, and now I'm seeing everything overlaid with a rainbow of emotion. Is that chastisement in h'Rawd's aura? Actual *chastisement*, staining the psionic plan a pink-ish yellow. I take a good look at Dude and—

My heart freezes up. Dude's different from other critters, able to do things that he shouldn't. I've known that for a while, had it hammered home when he found his way into the Aer, the dream space where the kin create their own version of Jørn but this... The bright golden halo surrounding the fuzzball has the strength of a sun. It's too bright to look at, and it radiates from his core, the edges fading to a tear-inducing orange.

Not even Onah has an aura like that. Not even the Regan, glimpsed in the dramatisation of training memories burned as bright as this genetically-engineered janitor barely the size of two clenched fists.

At some point while I floated in the stasis unit/escape pod and the years in the wherever-the-fuck-it-was, Aeotu gave me fug-feet, Dude got an upgrade.

A serious upgrade.

Fuck.

From the way shock is spilling around h'Rawd's paws - a

colourless sparkly wave – I'm guessing he's thinking the same thing.

Dude jumps off the rucnart's face onto my shoulder.

H'Rawd's gaze follows, and still that sparkle is spilling around his paws, but turning solid, shock becoming consideration. All four of his eyes meet mine, and he stares at me.

Double fuck.

I don't move. Don't even bolster my shields, don't breathe. Don't do anything save gather every last speck of myself and hold it close, ready to run.

In the face of certain annihilation it is the only appropriate response, or at least, that's what I'm telling myself. The fug has other ideas. I can feel it crawling over my body, thickening around my neck, my fingers lengthening into claws.

*Go.* H'Rawd's voice booms in my head, a command sphere unfolding along with it, planting instructions in my brain. I don't know exactly what's in it, but purpose ripples down my spinal cord, makes my feet itch with the need to move.

I'm guessing there's another part of the command sphere keeping my mouth shut, bottling up the questions that want to burst out of me, because I'm silent as h'Rawd wraps his forelegs around h'Lott's unconscious form and lifts her.

As soon as her weight is gone, I scoot backward, the command pressing me to move, but still I can't quite—

*They need to see you*, he says.

"You" is loaded with meaning, an image of Kuma, the boy I was before, and a separate one, of me as I am now, a strange amalgamation of fug and flesh. There's something else there too, a hidden meaning, but… "They" has just exploded on my brain, carrying an image of crew, of Mum and Dad huddled over a workbench, a huge holo lighting up the centre.

Really, h'Rawd shoulda just led with that.

# CHAPTER FIVE

H'Rawd's command sphere leads the way, directing my feet through Aeotu's broken corridors to an access tube. At least, I'm assuming it's a tube, h'Rawd thought it was.

The tube looks pretty much the same as the rest of the alien ship, a little skinnier maybe, a little rounder, but the sides still move with the same shifting patterns, whorls blending into lines, into circles. Like before, the awareness is trying to untwist them, whispering the possibility of meaning; it's enough to give me a headache.

The end of the tube is in front me before my head has time to explode. One moment I'm staring at a solid bulkhead, the next it's a translucent bit of skin, power running through it like blood, and then it's *snapped* into the deck and I'm walking through a double hand-width section of steelcrete, the metal pock-marked and holey. Fug-eaten.

I'm on the edge of what used to be Engineering, the topmost of *Citlali's* decks, excluding the little pimple that is the Attrium. It's the pile of metal and the skeleton of what used to be a work shuttle that give it away, the rest of the space…

The rest of the deck is full of holes and the remnants of spaces that might have been familiar once but are now alien, and not in the way Aeotu is, with its carved bulkheads and curved ceilings.

This is worse. This is the familiar warped and broken, a ruin where once was smooth steelcrete and colourful holos.

What happened? I need to talk to Core now more than ever, to know what happened in the time before I woke up. Before I was ejected into space, the fug had been repairing *Citlali,* making her whole.

The awareness has no answers, but deep in the back of my brain, in the place where the sticky web of darkness came from, is the memory of battle, of critters spreading disease. Of kin and humans walking through *Citlali's* corridors, spewing fire.

It makes my heart stop, my head light. I want to know, want to see the faces of the people, want to know when and how and *where.* Where are they now? Why didn't they come find me? And lastly, most importantly—

'How long was I out?'

I'm getting sick of the way my voice echoes, bounces from strut to the hole in the decking, repeating over and over and over. Getting sick, too, of the lack of answers.

Maybe, just maybe now that I'm aboard *Citlali,* and if there are crew awake… 'Core!'

*Core. Core. Core.*

'Core! Answer me!'

*Core. Answer. Core. Answer.*

I'm drawing in breath for another yell, feeling those too-big lungs like a mirage, when the air shimmers. It's not much, a flicker of gold over the lacy remnants of a bulkhead. It flickers again, bright sparks in the darkness, and is gone.

Breath burns in my lungs as I wait for it to come back.

Nothing.

I release the breath in a rush.

Typical.

H'Rawd's command sphere nudges the back of my brain, moving me forward. It guides me around piles of debris, through twisted bulkheads to a hole in the deck.

It's as wide across as I am tall, and black as the void; there's no way to tell how far down it goes. It could be just a couple of metres or all the way through the ship. It probably hasn't ruptured the outer hull though, or this whole section would be in vacuum. Still, jumping down it doesn't seem like the smartest idea, although... There's that whisper, the awareness telling me it's safe, that it's the best way to find the others. What decides me is Dude, his front paws perched on my chest as he looks over the edge of the hole and then back to me, expectation clear on his fuzzy little face.

I bounce a little on my fug-feet, feeling the springiness, the strength in the turned-back ankle. Take a deep breath. The memory of another tube, of my grav-belt failing, rings in my brain. Another breath.

Dude *fuzzes.*

'Whatever. I guess I've done dumber things.'

I jump.

Turns out, jumping down the hole wasn't the stupidest thing I've ever done, and that my fug accessories are tough, like, really tough. So tough, I hardly felt the impact, and hey, look Mum, no broken bones!

I take it as a win, even though I have no idea where I am. I might have started on Engineering, which, given the lack of bones poking through my skin, should have meant I was on one of the two Lab decks right below it, but this place looks more like Medical – a lot of plasglas walls and dark blue deck plating. What there is of the bulkheads is a soothing pale grey. That would mean I dropped three decks, nine metres straight down with the gravity on and I'm walking away like it was just a short hop off a table.

If it weren't so fucking freaky, my fug-self would be cool.

The last time I was on Med deck, it was choked with fug. The corridors might be clear of it, but the scars on the bulkheads and the holes in the deck show where it once was. As I make my way deeper into the level, the fug signs fade.

Most of the bulkheads on Med's inner rings are intact, with the occasional scorch or claw mark. A few places are honeycombed with holes, the steelcrete reduced to thin filaments of itself. The signs of fighting are heaviest around those areas, the walls black with char, the deck thick with what *looks* like dust, if dust was a dull, grey-green colour.

The dead fug puffs up around my feet, coating my legs to the knee, *sticking* there and... Is it my imagination, or is the me-fug absorbing it? As I watch, the dull patina on my shins fades and the stuff covering my thighs reaches fractionally higher.

'Okay.' I look up and concentrate on the junction ahead. 'Okay,' I say again, ignoring the squishy, sick sensation in the back of my throat. Focus on the things I can control, like getting from here to wherever it was h'Rawd wanted me.

It would have been nice if h'Rawd had included a little more in the way of actual directions instead of this vague pull of *home*, but whatever. I'll take what I can get.

At the junction, the pull drags me toward the left and the outer rings, away from Med's inner workings, where the heart of the Medical units and Command are, but... There's a new sensation tickling the back of my mind, another tug coming from my gut, telling me to go right, deeper into the core of what used to be *Citlali's* nerve centre.

The only place more protected than Command and central Med labs was Core, where *Citlali's* AI lived. Lives. Where she *lives*. I saw that flicker on the bulkhead, remember?

A little bit of me, the bit that holds back all the shit I've seen, that bit is telling me to grow up and stop believing that any of this is going to be all right, that someday I'm going to wake up and everything is going to be as it was.

That bit is a prick, and I'm ignoring him

I'm not ignoring the tug at my gut though, not now that Dude is sitting to attention, his little nose pointed in the same direction as that tug.

It guides me first down one corridor and then another, turning left and then right until I'm staring at what used to be main sickbay, the place I spent a couple of days healing up after I entered the ora for the first time. Where I first talked to Aeotu and where I launched an assault on the fug. That place. It looks different from the outside, different from how it used to be. The plasglas walls are dark, not with soot but turned opaque by the AI.

The tug in my gut keeps me moving, turning away from the main lab and away from Command. The fug-dust gets thicker the farther I walk. It clings to everything, sticks in my nose, coats my lips, and even the me-fug is having trouble absorbing it. I skirt around the inner ring, and just as it seems like I've been walking forever, I stop.

Dude vibrates with tension and his fur – dulled to a dirty yellow by the dust – stands on end. His ears are flat to his head and all four of his eyes are fixed on the door in front of me.

It doesn't look like much. I've passed any number of doors the exact same shade of middling grey, featureless, their corners rounded. Before the fug, a holo would have popped up at eye-height, telling me what this room was for and who worked in it. Now, there's nothing save the ever-present charring and the fug-dust, a thicker coating here than anywhere else.

I guess a lot of fug died here, but why?

The important parts of the ship were closer to the centre of the deck – Command and Medical. Why fight over a lab on the outskirts of nowhere? Was there something in the decks above or below?

I'm looking at the deck like I can see through it. Stasis is below, and the fug had conquered that before Onah pushed me out of my pod. However long ago that was. The awareness is whispering numbers to me, but they're too big to be real.

The answer to why – why this lab, why do I feel the need to go inside – is behind the door. A door that doesn't budge no matter how I push or prod. The need to get in is building in my gut, it's not just the tug anymore or Dude all tense and silent on my shoulder, there's a stench on the psionic plane that whispers of the same wrongness that clung to the skeletons on Aeotu and raises the hairs on my nape.

It mixes with the frustration in my chest, acid to the base already there, and explodes out of my throat in a yell and shoots down my arm, my fist *cracking* into the door. Pain shoots up my arm, throbs in my knuckles, but it's distant, dulled by the head-sized spiderweb of cracks radiating from the impact.

I step back, look at it, look at my knuckles, at the thick ridges of fug forming over the bleeding skin. Turn my attention back to the door.

Huh. I wonder…

I ball up my hand, do it again. Without the yell this time.

Another *crack* and the spiderweb grows. And this time, even though I feel the impact jarring up my arm to my shoulder, there's no pain and the fug over my knuckles is thicker.

Cool.

Again and again I hit the door. With each strike the spiderweb grows, the cracks at the impact site growing bigger and bigger until the steelcrete begins to crumble.

A little bit of me, the prickish negative part, is telling me steelcrete shouldn't do that, shouldn't crack under the impact of a shuttle let alone a scrawny boy with fug on his hands. But I'm not looking a gift critter in the mouth, this door is coming apart, and whether or not it's because I suddenly have superpowers or the fug is eating the metal, I don't care.

Even Dude agrees with me. There's excitement in the tension holding his body still, an edginess vibrating from his paws.

One last blow and I'm through, my shoulder slamming up against the door as my fist punches out the other side. The hole widens as I pull my arm out, the metal crumbling, chunks raining down around my feet, thudding into my fug-toes. My hand hasn't even cleared the door before Dude is scampering down my arm and leaping into the darkness beyond.

'Hey! Wait up!'

There's no answer, not even a chitter.

It takes a few more punches before the space is big enough for me to follow, and even then I have to suck in my gut and squeeze.

The lab beyond is small and dark, less lab than observation corridor. No workbenches, no hover stools, nothing except giant biotanks running down either side. The tanks have a faint glow, almost enough to see by but not enough to stop me from catching the fug-paws on the hoses snaking over the floor.

I have a nice up-close view from my place face-down on the deck. There's something strange about the hoses, it's nothing I can see – I mean, it's a *tube* – but the hairs on my nape are on end again. I can practically smell the wrongness I sensed outside, an old musty smell like that time I forgot to activate the cyclers and our shipsuits grew enough mould to make fug jealous.

A small *thud* on my back and Dude's fuzz is flooding my system, except instead of the calming gold I've come to expect from him, this is a jagged, unhappy buzz, and it's directed at the tanks.

I push myself up, and get my first real good look at them.

The biotanks are huge – floor to ceiling sheets of plasglas holding back enough biogel to drown a shuttle – and whatever's in them is the source of the wrongness. I concentrate on the crawling sensation, and... It's not kin, although it has the sense of a rucnart, the sharp bite of their minds. It's not Jørgen either, doesn't jump and jiggle like the rest of us human psions. There's a *snap* there, a creeping hiss that reminds me of the fug.

Maybe because there's a thin layer of the stuff frosting the tank.

My hand hovers over the plasglas with its thin carpet of fug, and even with my fug-hands, I can't quite bring myself to touch it.

Whatever this stuff is, it's different, even fug-me can sense it. The stuff winding around my fingers has retreated, leaving Kuma flesh to hover over the plasglas. The fug on the tank hardly even looks like fug, it's... Ordered, a geometric lacework crawling over the plasglas.

And there's more fug *inside* the tank.

A mouldy geometric carpet of it, vine-like ropes coiled on the bottom, twisting upward through the liquid, powerlines wound through them – brilliant blue veins of energy throbbing in time with an artificial heart. And the fug itself is a different colour, not the grey-green that covers my hands and feet, but a yellow-gold that reminds me of gelpaks and Core hovering over a workbench, of Dude sitting in a box as the Med AI fixed him.

Shadows are suspended in the tank, connected by the fug-lines; little blobs of darkness the size of my fist. Hundreds of them lined up in evenly spaced rows. I press closer, trying to peer through the murk, and think I can make out miniature paws, sleek bodies and pointed muzzles. They look like critters, all sleeked out, like Dude without his fuzz, but there's something off about them, something about the points of their muzzles, the paddles on the ends of their feet, and their heads... You can't really make out a critter's head amongst all the fluff, not unless you really look, and since they're always scurrying about, only stopping long enough to clean up the latest spill, that's not easily accomplished. Still... I've spent enough time with Dude that the flatness of their heads, without the tiny bump of their eye ridges, strikes me as off, like they don't have eyes. But then how do they see?

There are more shadows behind the first rows, fainter, and I wonder how deep the tank goes, how many critters are growing in there.

Dude's still huddled on my shoulder, still emitting that wobbly fuzz.

'It's okay, Dude. They're just critters, like you.' Except I'm lying, whether to myself or to Dude it doesn't matter. There's that sense of wrongness about the tank, about the yellow-gold fug. It grates along my spine, trying to find a place to lodge in my psyche.

The wise part of me, the bit that sounds like Mum telling me not to touch the holofire when I was three years old, is whispering that slipping into the eter and investigating the wrongness is a bad idea. The rest of me... I'm already in, leaving my body behind for the endless white of the psionic plane, and I'm reaching out and pulling that grating sensation with me.

One moment I'm all alone in the eter, and the next I'm staring at the biotank. The shadows are no longer shadows but balls of yellow-gold, calm and sleepy, barely aware. There aren't as many as I thought, a few hundred, in fact... I twist the tank in my mind, shrinking it until I can see the whole thing. There are gaps in the field of critters, blank spots disrupting the even spacing. Dead critters? Embryos that didn't make it? Without seeing a report, it's hard to tell.

That's not what's grating along the inside of my head though, that's something else, something that even here, is eluding my sight.

The spark is what gives it away, yellow-gold lightning forking between the shadows. I've seen that before, know it like I know how to slip through the threads of reality and find the other place, the place where Aeotu lives. The ora, Grea called it.

Where the eter is an endless field of white, the ora is everything and nothing all at the same time. There is no light, no colour, no time. There is just possibility. Infinite. Unending. It's like being in the cradle of the universe, where galaxies are made. And it's dangerous. All too easy for me to lose myself – to kill myself – hunting shadows.

The first time I came here, chasing the fug, Aeotu was a mirage on the very edges of my reach. A vibration felt more than seen, and so far away I almost died trying to find her. Now... Now Aeotu is everywhere. The ora is no longer empty but filled with the kaleidoscope of her being, blazing like a sun.

But she isn't the source of the grating against the inside of my ears. That's different, carried on the yellow lightning zapping over my skin.

*Sister.* Aeotu's voice shivers through the darkness.

I slap it away.

*I'm not your sister. I'm not even a girl.* Girl bits notwithstanding.

A pause. I can feel her considering me, considering too the space around me, the *wrongness* against my skin and then… Anger. Fear. It lashes out, not at me but at the *wrongness*. The wave blasts over me, powerful enough to rip the skin from my bones.

It's gone and my flesh is still attached but the lightning is no more.

*Safe.* Aeotu's whisper ripples through the eter, and I think... I think that she was protecting me.

*What was it?*

Nausea punches me in the gut, the sense of small angry teeth gnawing on my bones, of a fog rolling through my thoughts turning part of my brain numb. *Illness,* Aeotu says. *Given.*

"Given" is violent, rips a hole in my chest and shoves the grating in. A cold wriggling ball of sickness that feels like pieces of kin, Jørgen and Aeotu held together with cherry—

Lightning wraps around my ribs, yanks me out of the ora, but not back into my body.

Grea stands in front of me, her hands in my chest, wrath scrunching her face, baring her teeth.

I rip her hands out.

'Shit, Grea!' A mental projection or not, my chest feels like Grea punched through bone and muscle and stuck a subline into my heart. 'That hurt!'

She grabs my face, squishing my cheeks together. 'Are you okay?'

Once again, I push her away. 'I *was* until you decided to jumpstart my central nervous system.'

'What'd Aeotu want?' It's less a question than a demand, hiding a spark of desperation.

'I don't know, she was just there.' I rub my chest, trying to ease the cramp forming where her hands were. 'Don't you have a mainline to her or something?'

Grea looks different. There's a nimbus, a dark mirage around her body that shadows her every movement from hands to toes, it's darker around her shoulders though, seeming to flow from them. She's looking over my shoulder, eyes distant, teeth gnawing on her lower lip.

'Grea?'

She keeps chewing, still not looking at me.

'Grea!'

She glares at me, but it's distracted, her eyes unfocussed. 'What?'

'Where are you?' And I'm not talking about her physical location, but where she is now, mentally.

Is it my imagination or does Grea's mirage whisper?

She nods, and her gaze snaps to me, pinning me to the spot. 'You gotta find me, Kuma. Don't trust Aeotu, don't trust anyone. Just find me.'

She's gone before trepidation has finished freezing my spine.

# CHAPTER SIX

The command sphere leads me through Stasis.

Nightmares walk these corridors. My nightmares. I half expect them to crash through the fug-eaten bulkheads. In a way it would be better if they did, would give me something to do other than wonder if my friends were behind those walls, corpses rotting to dust.

There's a stasis unit ahead, the hatch cracked and shoved aside, the bulkhead around it showing signs of fug damage, holes through which the blue light of emergency shields glows. A neon glow in the darkness.

I can't sense anyone inside, no sheen of emotion, not even the jangle of another psion. There's no reason I should go in there, nothing but the pull in my stomach and the memory of Captain Lyn.

It should put me off, that memory, of her hand reaching through dried biogel and the rancid stench of decay. It should, but it doesn't.

I have to know.

I hesitate on the threshold, just beyond the curve of the corridor, the hatch obscuring my vision. Do I really want to do this? That little voice in my head says, "Yes".

Okay then.

There's no real memory of walking through the hatch, just the impression of steelcrete held together by thin strands of metal, and then I'm inside, and the pods are right there. Four of them, standing side-by-side, their canopies clouded with dust, surrounded by fug hanging in thick strands, crawling over the covers and around the pods' bases. It's a veritable forest, a jungle, and my heart beats hard, waits for the fug to move, to come for me.

Dude is a reassuring hum on my shoulder, spreading waves of gold through my skin while the armour contracts around my arms, reminding me that it's there and it's not eating me.

There are little blooms of yellow-gold and pops of the same wrongness that permeated the bio-tanks. They're peeping out at me from the tangle of fug almost like they're trying to hide, and I think that's worse than the fug.

One of the pods stands open, empty, the space within lined with a fine layer of grey dust and a thin carpet of fug. The others... The fug's thicker around them, the wrongness with it.

Vines the width of my biceps wrap around the pods, piercing the canopies, where there's canopy left at all. Most are shattered, thick shards of plasform spewed over the deck, the dried remnants of biogel sunk through the grates, some still clotted on the steelcrete mesh. And inside... Bodies.

There's no smell. That thought hits me first, strikes me as weird in fact, makes me wonder if the air-cyclers here are working or if the fug mask is filtering the scent like it does the air. Probably. Either that... either that or the bodies are so old all the smell has left them, the bacteria that breaks down flesh dead and gone.

Except there's still flesh on those bodies, faces and hair and naked limbs wrapped in fug. My feet take me closer, fug-paws crunching on bits of plasform, not even registering the pain of the shards piercing flesh. It's not flesh, I remind myself. Still, I can feel it *crunch* so why can't I feel it cut?

It's not really the thought to be having, not the important thing staring me in the face, but it's better than what *is* staring me in the face. I didn't know Horn like I did Mac, or Jim Engineer or Mae Lu. Didn't know him more than to know he was a fiend of the speedway, always pushing to go faster, higher, further. I was there when he overrode the safeties on the freight system and rigged a palette to shoot out in the void and back again. Remembered the tension in the air when he docked and there was Captain Lyn, fury rolling off her like I never wanted to sense again, her face a meteor storm. He'd got off that palette, encased in an EVA suit and tried not to *look* like he'd just had the time of his life. Horn did a decent job of keeping the grin from his face, but couldn't help the exhilaration rolling off his psyche.

Couldn't even lock it down enough to prevent the captain from sensing it.

Even in death, it still looks like Horn is grinning, just not with his mouth.

Horn's neck is a dark, ragged mess.

There are claw marks in the flesh. Blood. Dried and old. Flaking. Fug doesn't kill like that, doesn't open flesh and expose bone. Fug doesn't leave anything behind except the desiccated skeletons of its victims. Skeletons that crumble at the slightest touch.

Kin killed Horn.

Kin.

I stand there, waiting for that to sink in, for what I'm looking at to make sense, to find a place in my brain. I'm standing there for a long time, waiting for enlightenment to strike.

I just...

Kin killed Horn.

It's not like I didn't know they'd killed other Jørgens, hadn't smelled the blood on h'Rawd's breath, but it doesn't stop the thought echoing in my brain, over and over and over. Bouncing off the sides of my skull even as I turn to the other pods. The rest of Horn's family was in here, his dad and mum. His aunt too. He didn't have any siblings, just them, and I guess only his aunt got out, 'cause the pods on either side of him are occupied. Although, I guess his mum could have got out, I didn't really know her that well either, and she looked a lot like her sister.

It's all moot at the moment. The only way I know Horn's dad didn't get out is because he's the only other one with a penis. His dad's face is gone, not just covered over or obscured, but gone, and the rest of his flesh isn't far behind. I can see bones and muscles and tendons, the thick rope of intestines spilling out of the hole in his belly. I'm pretty sure fug has done most of it, *is* doing most of it, but some of the holes... They look more like tears, like the ragged marks on Horn's throat.

The *awareness* is cataloguing the damage, highlighting parts of the body, outlining the claw marks, picking out lumps of yellow-gold and flooding my eyes with information, but I don't need it.

I don't need to see more.

This is enough to fuel my nightmares, to refill the spot where the image of Captain Lyn's hand had started to fade.

This is enough.

Enough knowledge, enough dread, enough anger.

I tromp out of the unit, pausing on the threshold, dragging air into my lungs. Just, standing there, taking it in. The corridor, the crumbled bulkheads, the fug, the glow of emergency shields, and the hatches. So many hatches, some standing open, some still shut. How many of them are filled with corpses? Were Horn's family the only ones the kin killed? And why?

Kin and human have shared *Citlali* for decades, have saved each other, helped each other. Been allies, if not friends, ever since the first exploration ship launched from Jørn. It was part of our purpose, part of the *reason* the ships had been built as they had, with organic and technological components. One species could not survive this journey without the other.

So why?

Like so much since I woke up, it doesn't make sense and the *awareness* in my gut isn't helping.

It's Aeotu who answers, reaching up through the awareness. Sorrow rides her hard, apology and guilt bringing up the rear. *Sisters*, she says and I have an impression of many kaleidoscopic minds connected one to the other in a sprawling network. The impression changes and the minds become restless balls of energy – Jørgen minds – shrivelling, rotting as she ties them into a new whole.

*Wrong*, she whispers.

# CHAPTER SEVEN

My spine stays frozen for a long time. All the way down through fug-eaten freight tubes and another hole in the deck. It's still with me as I squeeze through a crack that used to be a section of decking and is now an access hatch to the deck below.

I drop, fug-ankles absorbing enough of the impact that my knees barely need to bend, Dude not even wobbling from his perch on my shoulder.

If I have my bearings right and I haven't slipped through a wormhole to the other side of the universe, this is A/Rec One, the first of the accommodation and recreation decks where the crew lives when they're not in stasis/sleep. There's a clone of it below – A/Rec Two – where Mac used to live with his mum.

Used to live. Those words ring in my brain, pause my feet, and I wonder when I started thinking of Mac as dead, especially now I have proof that at least some of the crew live.

I shake it aside and keep walking. And finally, *finally* as I head deeper into the deck, the ice in my spine starts to thaw.

I know these corridors – the way the hatches fit into the curve of the corridor, with a new one every ten strides; the extra springiness in the decking that's supposed to make it more homey, but make you feel like the gravity's turned down instead – and yet they're strange to me.

There should be voices in the air, the gentle hubbub of people talking and laughing, the smell of pancakes. The bulkheads are scratched and grey, looking like the steelcrete they're made of rather than flowing with a shifting landscape of holos; scenes of fields and forests, interspersed with the never-ending human-made canyons of the floating cities and wild explosions of abstract colour.

Instead, all I hear is the grind of malfunctioning air-cyclers grating along my ears like the anger and grief grate along my brain. Harsh. Cold. Hopeless.

I hold the emotions back, shoring up shields and trying to ignore the dread gripping my insides. Dude helps, *fuzzing* his butt off in my shoulder, but the *NICK NICK* of the fug-claws are a boom in my ears and the sound of my breathing is hard, a gale rushing in and out of my nose.

There's light up ahead, the first glimmer of warmth. The awareness tells me there are heat signatures, but can't say more. There's something wrong with this sector of the ship, something keeping it out.

The light spills from an open hatch, staining the scarred grey decking a warm gold.

I stop in the shadows, the light a millimetre from my toes, heart beating hard, fighting back the hope and fear, making a mess of my breathing.

'...repaired the shielding around the faster-than-light engine but there's still not enough material to kickstart the fusion.' Jim Engineer, there's a new hardness to his voice, but I remember the deep, slow tones well enough. 'Without it, we're not going anywhere.'

'We'll scavenge it from the stasis generator.' Mac's dad. I picture him as he was the last time I saw him – short and broad, some of it fat, most of it muscle.

*And what about the crew still in their pods?* White around a core of boiling black, Onah projects his mental voice.

*Do you truly believe they live?* I recognise Mwat's voice. The female qwan's clipped, precise thoughts conjure the memory of her looking down her muzzle, inspecting me like a bug. *Stasis is* Their *domain.*

*Can we take the chance that our people do not?* Onah says.

'It's all moot unless we can sever the grappling cables.' Mum. My heart jumps in my chest. 'The viral slag laid by the neo-critters is sticking.'

'I thought the nanotech we reverse engineered from the alien ship wasn't functional?' Mac's dad says.

'It's functional now.' And now my heart stops a second time, because that's Dad's voice. 'Someone altered the programming.'

'Who?'

'Do you even need to ask?' That's Jim, his voice thick with anger. 'We should have dealt with her already.'

'The way you've *dealt* with the others?' Anger may have rolled in Jim's voice, but Dad vibrates with it, and he has just enough empath in him to make the air shake.

*They were in pain*, Onah's words drip with grief and the same guilt I sense in the dark place, before h'Rawd—

I cut the memory off.

'That's not the only reason.' Accusation joins the anger in Dad's voice, makes it thick and hard, has the weight of a grievance older than me.

'Jori…' Mum begins, and there's something in her voice, a hardness, a warning, that twigs that sense of wrongness.

'They were our friends, Aino. The *children* of our friends.'

'They weren't there anymore, their minds were gone,' she says.

'You don't know that.'

*But we do.* There's no emotion in Mwat's voice, only the weight of age and authority.

'And we're to trust you? Like we did with Arthur?'

*Your friend caused his own downfall*, Mwat says.

'Arthur Tudor was part of this crew.' Dad's voice shakes. 'And *you* killed him for doing his job.'

Arthur Tudor. The name rings in my head, bouncing from side to side, conjuring a memory… Arthur *David* Tudor. AD. The beacon in Dad's lab, the *alien* beacon.

Oh shit.

I can almost imagine Mwat, the slow deliberate blink, first her lower eyes and then her upper, before she pins Dad with the full weight of her stare. *We are here because he went against our wishes.*

'How was he to know—'

*We told him.* Silence greets Onah's statement. *And still he connected with the beacon, as only an empath could.*

'It was a ruin, ancient. We weren't to know...' Dad's voice trails off, the heat gone from his words. 'She can't possibly know...'

I almost miss that last bit, the quiet anguish on the "she", 'cause I'm still reeling over the fact that AD Tudor was an empath, a freaking *empath*. Like me. Like Grea.

Everyone had always said we were the only ones...

'Jori—' A pause, and I imagine Mum putting an arm around Dad's shoulders, rubbing his arm. 'We'll figure it out.'

My head's still reeling but it doesn't stop me staring at that rectangle of light like if I concentrate enough, I can transport myself in there and see them, watch them, touch them. Just a few steps, a couple of metres and I could do it, could feel Mum's arms around *my* shoulders, breathe in Dad's warm scent, and just... Just what? Be me? Rewind until before the fug?

Pain radiates though my hands. I look down, at the claws piercing my palms, at the fug crawling over my skin, and then further, at my feet, at my bent-back ankles and three stubby toes, the talons gripping the deck.

I step back.

Dude chitters, tiny claws pricking my neck and sticks his nose in my ear.

I jerk, fug-feet tangling at the sudden movement, and stumble over the cables.

A crash.

The voices cut off.

My heart stops.

Boots pounding the deck, wings beating, a snarl.

The golden rectangle is full of shadows, people rushing out, light glinting off pistols and multi-tools.

And now I'm on my arse, staring up at familiar faces.

Dude hums.

Fear and anger saturate the corridor, turning the air thick with clouds of black and red before surprise, hope and horror blast it all away.

I get to my feet, careful to move slow.

'Kuma?'

'Hey Dad.'

'I—?' I'm enveloped in a hug. Arms wrapping around my shoulders, lifting my heels off the floor. I smell Dad, bury my nose in his shoulder, wrap my hands around his back and—

'Step away, Jori,' Jim says, pointing a pistol at my face.

Jim Engineer's expression is stone – cold and hard. And scared. Med-gel wraps around the lower half of his face, completely covering one cheek and half of his mouth, before slipping over his throat and disappearing under his shipsuit. The uncovered half of his face is... eaten, I guess. Pock-marked and massed with the white mesh of hastily regrown skin.

Pain radiates from him, a dark murky pink, and not just physical pain. There's grief tangled in it, void-dark strands threaded through every breath. It matches the emotion in his eyes. Jim had a partner, and I know without asking that Jess is dead.

Dad is turning, one arm around my shoulders, holding me close, confusion saturating his aura, and maybe a touch of outrage.

I step away, dropping my arms. One step, two, putting distance between us, 'cause I know what Jim Engineer has seen, and I know what Dad *hasn't* seen, hasn't realised, and I know it's not going to be good when he does.

Because I can see Mum, standing behind Jim, and she's seen. Her eyes are locked on my hands, are travelling up my arms, taking in my face, and when I move, her attention drops to my feet.

The light's not good here, casts stark shadows over noses and under brows, makes skin grey, but I don't need it. Mum's aura has gone sparkly with shock.

...and that step back she takes tells me everything.

'It's okay, Dad.' My too-deep voice is scratchy, squeezing past the lump in my throat. 'He's just worried.'

Dad whips back around and that thread of outrage in his aura is turning to anger. 'Kuma—'

I hold up my hands.

He stops.

Stares.

Sparks are going off in the air around him, the muddy grey of confusion giving way to disbelief, and then the bright orange of comprehension. He steps back too.

It's just a half-step and I know it's involuntary, that it's shock as much as instinct, because he takes it back immediately, reaches out to me, but it's still a knife in my heart.

I push him back.

'It's okay,' I say again, this time to Mum, half-hidden in the shadows behind Jim Engineer. 'It's not... eating me or anything. It's actually been kinda... helpful.' If helpful involved defending myself from h'Rawd and h'Lott. Of course, if I hadn't been half-fug, they probably wouldn't have attacked—

*He is part of* Them. Mwat's voice booms in my head, filling me with the echo of ancient training memories – rucnarts pursuing flat-nosed aliens down curving corridors. *You attacked the tree-kin, like* It *did.* A newer image; a dark, sleek figure cutting through tree-kin, blood flying from its talon-like fingers.

Hope fills my chest, chases out the questions about Horn and being "whole". 'There's someone else like me?'

The worst part about silence are the things that fill it. Dread fills this one, rising around my knees, cold and toxic, reeking of secrets and pain.

It makes my blood curdle.

There's a conversation going on that I can't hear, I can tell from the tiny frown over Dad's nose and the way Jim and Mum's eyes glaze. Onah's the only one whose expression doesn't change. 'Course, it's hard to read a qwan's face, the ridges between their upper and lower eyes always seem to be drawn in a frown and their muzzles wrinkled with distaste, for all I know, Onah is smiling.

'It's Kuma,' Mum says. 'It's my son. We take the chance.'

I'm not sure what chance they think they're taking. Fug-feet aren't contagious, at least that's what the awareness tells me, but the faces in front of me haven't got the same message.

Mwat. Mac's dad. Jim.

Their judgement hits me in the face.

Mum's the worst. She stands against the back wall of our old kitchen, arms crossed, no emotion stains her aura or her expression.

Dad echoes her pose but where the workbench separates me from her, Dad's a solid presence at my side, his protectiveness washing over me like a shield. Its strength hasn't diminished in the whole time I've been sitting here, recounting the events since Onah pushed me out of stasis/sleep, a lifetime ago.

*You told the AI to attack* Citlali, Mwat says.

'Not to attack—'

Jim doesn't let me finish. 'It's taken over *Citlali,* Kuma, how is that not attacking?'

Another breath. 'We're still here.'

'Here?' Jim is leaning across the table, pointing at his face. 'It killed my wife. I woke up and she was *dead*, Kuma!'

His grief pounds at my head and I feel like I should look away, should acknowledge his loss without challenging him but...

*He doesn't know loss,* my twin whispers in my head. With her presence comes anger, comes a harrowing loneliness, comes the sensation of death creeping slowly through my bones. It shoves me to the back of my own head and takes over my mouth, my face.

Grea is behind my eyes, twisting my lips, using my too-deep voice. 'It *ate* Mae Lu, he saw it carrying her parts away, *he* tried to do something.' She pushes me away from the bench, stalking around it, ignoring Dad and Mum and Onah as she/I advance on Jim, singling him out like a rucnart on the hunt. 'What'd you see? What'd you do? What'd you feel?'

She/I are in his face, and it's strange to notice that I'm taller than the man who used to ruffle my hair and tease me about being a shrimp. In the part of my brain not in shock over Grea's invasion, I wonder how much of it is because of the fug-feet and how much is me.

Jim's face is pale, the ridges of his scars white, while anger and not a little fear radiate from him. He opens his mouth, but Grea/I are poking him in the chest, and there must be more force behind it than I think, because it slams him against the bench.

'You did nothing,' Grea/I say. 'You saw nothing, you felt nothing because you were asleep in your little pod while *we* were saving your lives.'

Jaws are wide open, surprise, confusion and shock saturating the room, a miasma thick enough it's almost visible.

'Kuma, what's going on?' Dad is the first one to find his voice.

*Kuma does not speak.* Onah stands straight and tall. *Hello Grea. We have been trying to find you.*

Grea's/my eyes narrow, and although she/I direct our words to the qwan, her/my finger doesn't move from Jim's chest. 'I know, but I don't need your idea of help.'

I want to know what she means by that.

*You already know*, Grea says. *You've already seen it, felt it.*

The teeth in the dark. H'Lott's hot breath in my face. The stench of blood. Horn's ruined throat.

'Grea? Sweetheart?' That's Mum, reaching up to cup our face in her hands. 'Is that—'

Grea/I pull away, and this time the sneer on her/my face is full of teeth and anger. 'Don't think I don't know, Ma, don't think I didn't *see*, that I wasn't there. It was your idea,' she whispers.

Mum shrinks, and if I thought Jim's face was pale, Mum's is

bloodless, turning her golden complexion a strange shade of beige.

Guilt. Sadness. Anger. Fear. Suddenly I'm swamped in it, drowning in emotions, buried under their weight – Onah's, Mum's, Jim's. Everyone but Dad's and Mwat's.

They're stoic, pillars of nothingness in the midst of the torrent.

Even Grea is flooding me with the sweet, heady sense of victory, except... It's not just *her* emotion, there's a darker red to the cherry of her presence, a shadow like the one I sensed before.

In my gut, the *awareness* stills, recognition blooming. I'm reaching for the darker red, stretching like Mum reaching for Grea's/my cheeks, hope in her eyes.

There's a jerk, Grea's attention on me, a moment of alarm and then she's gone, taking the dark red with her.

# CHAPTER EIGHT

I'm left with questions and my own sorry self. Literally.

After Grea's outburst, everyone melts away; Mwat and Jim Engineer wasted no time letting our door swoosh shut behind them. Mum takes a little longer, stares at me.

I wait for her to say something, to explain what Grea meant, where her anger came from, but she leaves without a word.

Dad follows, squeezing my shoulder as he goes, his eyes on Mum and determination in the set of his jaw.

And so I'm left with questions; about Jim, about Mum, about Grea. Questions piling upon questions and no answers in sight. Just a holo rotating over the kitchen bench, rotating a fraction of a millimetre a second, like it's caught in molasses. There's something familiar about its form, two egg-shaped blobs melded together, the bottom one a third of the size of the top. It's not until I get closer that I start to make out what it is, sorting out the rounded point of a bow and the flat protrusions of the engine ports. Part of it, the bit that's being swallowed by the bigger egg, reminds me of *Citlali*, the way the underside swoops upward to meet the nose.

I pad closer until I'm leaning on the bench, getting as close to the holo as I can without sticking my head in it. There're the maintenance tubes that run around *Citlali's* middle, and there, just below the bulge where the bigger egg swallows the smaller, is the indentation that marks the upper shuttle bay.

Eight red spheres pulse on the smaller blob, three on each of the long sides and one each on the top and bottom of the egg. Thin lines trail from each, connecting it to the bigger egg, like the legs of some weird space arachnid holding onto prey.

My brain's still trying to come to grips with what my eyes are processing, and it takes studying the other egg, seeing the lines in its sides, the whorls that don't appear to do anything but make me want to follow them deep into their centre, for understanding to dawn

The small egg reminds of *Citlali* because it *is Citlali*, and the red bits are... Grappling cables, the knowledge comes from the *awareness* in my gut, pulling images of giant hooks buried deep in *Citlali's* hull, the ends growing, morphing to become part of the superstructure. Which would make the bigger egg, the one with the whorls...

'Aeotu,' I whisper.

*Sister.*

I jerk back.

It was just in my head. Just in my head.

And not in my head psionically, but a figment of my imagination. I'm telling myself that, but it's not comforting; makes my insides curl and my breath come short, 'cause, Old Terra. It's bad enough when it's Aeotu talking to me, reaching out over the psionic plane or creeping into my comms, but now I'm psyching myself out. Now I'm *letting* her in.

And she sounds like Grea.

That's what makes it really scary. What makes my insides shrivel and cold take over my guts. The dream-memory of being curled up with Grea, Aeotu behind her eyes, the darkness, and remembering the darker red in her presence when she took over my mouth. Not Aeotu but something *like* Aeotu.

When did the darkness behind her eyes change? When did Aeotu become Aeotu-but-not? So much has changed in the time I was asleep, least of all me.

Betrayal is a sour emotion, one that wraps around your heart and makes it curdle until the blood in your veins has spikes aimed right at the beating muscle. It's not something I've experienced much, not an emotion I've ever tried to foist on others, but I've sensed it, floating on the wind. Before we went into stasis/sleep, it had clung to Jim's partner. I'd brushed up against it, but hadn't gone further. Hadn't wanted to.

I don't want to feel this, don't want the weight of it in my chest when I think of my twin coming to me in the escape pod, starting this whole thing, and yet...

*I'm sorry.* Grea speaks in the back of my head, and for a moment, she's hovering over the kitchen bench, a ghost flickering within the mess of Aeotu devouring *Citlali*.

And she is, for the most part. *Why'd you do it?* I ask.

*I told you; you were leaving me.*

I shake my head. *It's more than that. You said we were going to live forever. What'd you mean?*

The ghost cocks her head. *Don't you want to live forever?*

*I want to know what you meant by it.*

*I meant what I said.*

*People don't live forever, Grea. It's biologically impossible.*

Grea frowns. *Why are you arguing with me fathead?*

*I just...* I can't answer. There is no answer, except that I feel it, deep within, coming from the place where the awareness sleeps, the knowledge that Grea is keeping something from me. *You're not telling me everything.*

*I don't have to tell you everything. You're my brother, not my conscience.*

*Why'd you say that?*

*Say what?*

*That I'm not your conscience?*

There's no answer. Silence rules the psionic plane and the ghost on the kitchen bench freezes, like a holo vid on pause. A smudge of vomit-green stains the bench at Grea's feet and I realise I'm seeing her on the eter, that I've half-slipped onto the psionic plane without knowing it, and as soon as that knowledge lights up my brain, I notice other things.

Things like the guilt Grea is struggling to cover up, trying to pull back into herself, and Dude, all sleeked out on my shoulder, tiny fangs bared.

If I thought Aeotu sounding like my twin had frozen my gut before, I was wrong. The guilt at Grea's feet makes my whole body cold, turns me into a void-frozen block of Kuma meat. *What have you done?*

*Nothing.* Except her answer is rich with lies, black curling through the vibrant cherry strands that make up her psyche.

I don't tell her not to lie, my disbelief does it for me, colouring the eter, a thick bronze, reaching out to Grea.

Again, silence wraps around my frozen sister. A barrier becoming thicker and thicker with every beat of our hearts, until it's visible, a solid wall of air. Cutting us off, doing all it can to strangle the connection that is us.

*I'll find out,* I say.

*You should worry less about me and more about Ma.*

Grea's trying to distract me with that, to stop me from chasing the lie. I should ignore it, I know I should but—

*What about Mum?*

*It was her idea to kill them.* An image of Horn, the wrongness clinging to him, his torn throat.

Grea smiles, the stretch of her lips thin, teeth sharp points, and starts to fade, her ghost becoming thinner. She's a mirage before I know what's happening, there and not.

*Grea!* I dive after her, leaving the physical world behind, Dude coming with me.

The wall she built is still there, thick and tall, blocking my way. I pound against it, throwing determination into the bricks along with my fists. It doesn't move, and behind it, the sense of Grea fades further.

*No. No. No. No.* Every denial is a strike against the barrier, an explosion of the emotions I've tucked into the pit of my being. Of anger. Of terror. Of the heart-stopping fear that everyone and everything I've ever loved is dead and gone. There's betrayal in there as well, the viscous stuff of it coating my knuckles, forming spiky ridges like a psionic version of the fug-armour.

The fug-armour.

I look down, and there it is, a shadow over my body. Pulsing with power. Power I can feel, like the too-big lungs. A great well of it rising up from my feet, coming from the place where the awareness lives. It rushes through my skin, a miniature sun at my command.

A thought, and it's pouring through my bones, forming a bright molten gauntlet above my fist. I flex my fingers, regard the barrier and strike.

The wall shatters, but Grea is gone. There's a trace of her left behind, a kind of psionic footprint, and in it there's a shimmer of emotion that doesn't belong. That's Aeotu-but-not. The memory is hazy, slipping out of my reach.

I wrap my hands in the stuff, but they slip through, like the red isn't there except—

A hand on my arm. Not Grea's. It's barely human, almost black but with a hint of something, green maybe, and shiny. Smooth, like liquid metal with shapes moving under the surface, shadows upon shadows. Light gleaming in dark green highlights. Five fingers ending not in neatly clipped nails or the fug talons that cover my own, but in long sharp spikes, seamless from knuckle to wicked end. It's attached to a wrist covered in the same liquid shiny, then an arm, a shoulder, a neck, a— A face? There's a head, as smooth as the rest of it, things that might be ears protruding from the sides in little bumps. I recognise the shape of a jaw, the dome of a skull, the lines and hollows of the tendons and collarbones that hold it up, even the bump of an Adam's apple, but the rest?

There's no nose, no mouth, no eyes. If Core had no physical features, if her avatar where the colour of midnight under a forest canopy, it'd look like this. Featureless. Freaky as fuck.

It's an up-close-and-personal look at the figure from Onah's memories; the dark, sleek being that cut through the tree-kin. There's more to it though, something that halts the panic rising in my chest, that spreads a familiar wave of warmth through it. A scent of... cumin and oranges and the indescribable shimmer of power that I've only ever sensed from one person.

I peer closer, try to peel back the layers of the eter and see under their skin. For a moment it feels like there's something reaching back, struggling to push through the shapes moving under the shiny surface.

'Mac?'

Joy. It's short. A brief spark of pink caught out the corner of my eye, sparkling under the thing's grip on my shoulder, and then it's gone. Disappeared like it never was, and all that I'm left with is... nothing. The eter is empty of emotion, or thought. Just me and Mac/not-Mac standing here, only his grip assuring me that this is real—

Pain. My pain. Mac's finger-spikes driving into my flesh, then feathers and fangs and the chilling scree of a qwan and then Mac is gone, vanished before I've had a chance to draw breath.

In his place is a storm of talons and lashing tails, of the musk of kin, storming around me, over me and then they too are gone, leaving blood, rage, and Onah in their wake.

The qwan stands in front of me. Tall. Proud. The dark purple feathers of his crest standing on end, both sets of wings partially spread, like he's going to take flight at any moment. Or he's just really, really pissed off.

*It came to you.* It's an accusation, the white/black of Onah's suspicion driving a knife thrust at my mind, the point sticking in my shields, trying to get through. *Why?*

I stumble. 'It was Mac, my best friend.' The words are out of my mouth, are flying through the air, my own daggers aimed at Onah's heart.

They're struck from the air, thrown back at me along with a fresh wave of suspicion, another assault against my shields. *It is not your friend.*

'It is, I *felt* him.' I grip Onah's knife in both hands. It's a thing of pure thought, shaped by my own imagining of it, given weight and substance by Onah's intent. Touching it is like reaching into the air-kin and wrapping my hands around his anima, or a pale imitation of it. It vibrates with the essence of him – white around a boiling darkness – rippling over my skin, pieces of it wrapping around my fingers, digging into my flesh like tiny talons.

Onah resists, pushes harder against the thin mental barrier that keeps the world separate, that keeps *me* private.

What Onah's doing is against kin law, against the rules that make it possible for psions to live with each other and not go insane. I'm straining to keep the tip from going deeper, arms straining, muscles from bicep to chest, to back to thighs, every fibre standing on end.

'Why are you doing this?' My voices shakes.

There's no answer, nothing save another push on the knife. He doesn't move but to draw his wings a little higher, to lean a little further forward, putting physical weight behind the psionic lance he's driving through my shields.

I push back, but I know, right in the heart of me, that it's not going to be enough.

Gold races over my hands on six tiny paws, leaps from the end of the knife. Dude flings himself in Onah's face, and if I thought Onah was a wrecking ball, Dude is an asteroid slamming into a planet.

Pieces of Onah fly, slamming into my shields, finding a crack.

I'm getting all too used to fear, the heft of it, the way it seeps between your thoughts. This fear has the soft, sly glide of secrets and the rotten stench of old shame. It brings with it a fragment of memory, flashes of AD Tudor sitting with the beacon in his lap, red encasing his hands and crawling over his chest. Darkness forms a cowl around his neck. There's something linked to the darkness, a knowledge passed from generation to generation, ringing with the dual lights of time and desperation.

Understanding is right there, obscured by the desperation, and I know that if I could just reach through and touch it—

Dude rockets into me, pushing me out of the eter.

I'm slumped against the kitchen bench, my arse on the floor, legs sprawled out before me. I've got a good view of my fug-feet from here, a real chance to study the play of tendons under the grey-green skin. When did the fug-feet get tendons? And while I'm on that, when did my toes start to look like toes? Longer and thinner, still three of them, still with the black tips of claws at the end; not human, not even close, but no longer quite as emu-like.

There's a hum from my shoulder, the soft brush of fur against my cheek, and I'm looking up, steering my mind away from the horror-wonder of my changing self to what's on the other side.

Dad's crouched in front of me. His shipsuit needs an injection of nanites, the fabric over his knees is thin, and the bottom of his cuffs where they brush the top of his boots, frayed. Concern is rolling off him, a gentle wave of pale blue butting up against my feet. Against my feet and not my head because he's crouched a half-metre away. A half-metre of the universe between him and me, between the joy I felt when he hugged me to the cold that lodges in my heart and grows.

And behind him... behind him are the others. Mum and Jim Engineer, Onah and Mwat all of them staring at me. Jim's got his hand on Mum's shoulder, holding her back, but she's not fighting that hard. There's an extra metre of distance between her and Dad, an extra ocean to cross.

That cold thing in my chest, I'm not going to let it hurt, not going to let it grow. Not going to let it twist and turn and become the hot, resentful thing lurking right in the depths of my being.

'Kuma?' Dad's reaching out to me, and while it looks like he's crossing that ocean of distance, he's pushing reluctance ahead of him. 'Are you back?'

My gaze darts behind him, to the kin and to Onah. His upper eyes are open, a hot orange. Warning flashes in them, a hint of the anger and pain that saturated the eter.

I can't help but look at Mum, can't help but see Horn's face laid over hers, can't help the echo of Grea's accusation.

*It was her idea.*

I don't want to believe it, to *think* it. It makes me sick, makes me want to curl in on myself and scream, but I guess I know the meaning behind Grea's words when she took over my mouth, what made Mum's complexion pale.

'Yeah,' I say, slowly turning my gaze back to Dad. 'I'm back.'

And I'm pissed, and that pissed-off-ness feeds the resentment brewing in my gut.

Dad inches forward, his hand still out, and I can feel his desire to help me, but that reluctance sours it. 'What happened?' he says.

I get my fug-feet under me and rise, ignoring the hand. 'I felt Grea.' A half-truth feels safe, easy and responsible. But I'm looking at Mum again, seeing Horn, and under it all... I meet Onah's gaze again. He's closed his upper eyes, and his lower ones, a rich deep green, are dark with caution and not a little fear.

On my shoulder, Dude growls, so low I doubt anyone but me can hear, and it's like he's echoing the nasty thing in my gut, the resentment and anger, all the stuff I've been denying. And I just want to get rid of it, to make everyone feel like this; so they *know*, so they understand.

My lip twists, my nose following and I picture my face twisted in a snarl to make h'Rawd jealous.

A throat clears, and Dad's rising, frustration fighting with anger in his eyes.

He holds out his hand. 'Kuma, we've been talking. About how to help you.'

Dad's good at keeping his emotions in check, not as good as Mum, but pretty decent, good enough that what he's feeling doesn't pound at my brain. And usually, usually I'm polite enough not to pry, but what worked before – before the fug and Aeotu – what worked then doesn't now.

Dad wouldn't hurt me, Mum would either, or Onah or even Mwat, but there's deception in Dad's words.

Deception has a strange flavour, it doesn't really taste like anything, just kinda slides over your tongue, a ghost of a favoured desert, or the scent of a treasured memory, saying 'look over there, remember that'. It's different from person-to-person, changing with their intent, but always leaving a silvery trail in its wake.

As a kid, it took me awhile to figure it out. Maybe if AD Tudor had been alive, I'd have caught on quicker.

I ignore Dad's outstretched hand, keeping my back to the kitchen bench, away from the lies and resentment in front of me.

The *awareness* whispers, *{{ Danger. }}*

Yeah. I know, and it makes my heart ache.

It's Mwat who speaks first. *Something speaks to you, little kin.* She fluffs her wings and waddles around the table, her tail dragging on the deck. *What is it?*

Pressure against my skull, tells me that she's trying to send more than words into my brain. I push her off.

'Get out of my head.'

*You are full of secrets.* There's no accusation in Mwat's tone, just curiosity.

'I guess I fit right in then.' And now I'm staring Onah in the eye, not the lower ones, but the upper. A kin's upper eyes are portals to their eter, and meeting them is akin to shoving your way into their mind and daring them to put you back in your place with teeth and talons.

Doing it now feels dangerous, feels like an invasion of privacy and respect, but you know what? I don't care. None of the kin seem terribly shy about invading *my* privacy, and the only respect I've found is at the end of my fug blades. It's time for a little turnabout, time for me to stand on my own two fug-feet and shove all the things *I've* done for the *Citlali* in their scared, ungrateful faces.

Onah blinks, upper lids sliding closed, the gesture the same as a human looking away.

A cheer echoes from the back of my mind, carried on a wave of cherry. Grea.

The warmth of it gives me the courage to turn the challenge on Mum. She's as close to a psionic null as anyone gets on *Citlali*, with just enough of the empath gene in her DNA to classify her as Jørgen. Challenging her to a psionic duel is about as effective as trying to light a fire in vacuum, and maybe that's what makes her so good at the stare-off.

She meets my gaze head on, and while there's guilt in her aura – still making my insides shrivel, despite Grea – there's no apology, no shame.

'Whatever your sister told you, Kuma, it had to be done.' Her voice is soft, but sure. It disturbs me more than the dismay that colours her aura every time she looks at me. Disturbs me because it feels so final, carries so much *conviction*.

I break the stare. Clear my throat. 'She says that it was your idea to kill my friends.'

'It was but I had a reason, a *good* reason.'

'What's so good about—'

There's a click, the awareness yelling {{ *Danger!* }}, Dude snarling, and a cherry-red bloom of fury so strong it knocks me off my feet. That's what saves me.

The energy bolt slams into the bulkhead where my head used to be.

No one moves, save Jim, re-aiming the pistol.

Of course, kin don't have to move.

*No.* Mwat has no hesitation, no finesse, she's a sledgehammer exploding through the psionic plane.

Jim Engineer vibrates in the qwan's psionic grip, tendons standing on end, muscles bulging, his rage bursting from his veins, unable to move.

*No*, Mwat says again. *Kuma is kin; we do not kill our own.* And now her gaze meets mine, red upper eyes unflinching and without challenge. An image of the place I woke up flashes between us. It's the first time I have actually seen it, the mounds of fug, the pale glimpses of hands and feet, the familiar faces. *We had our reasons for what we did. Not all of those taken were as you, not all were whole.*

There is more behind that, a whole solar system of memories held behind Mwat's eyes. I know without asking that she won't share.

*Go, little kin.* Mwat ruffles her feathers. *We will take care of this.*

There's nothing more to say, not with Jim's whole body shaking with the effort to shoot me.

I roll up off the deck and glide away.

# CHAPTER NINE

I stole a map on my way out of the A/Rec One, a water bladder and a jacket too, but I left the ration packs. Somehow, taking food didn't seem right, not when my stomach had yet to feel hunger and the thought of eating one of the tasteless, high-calorie bars made my tastebuds curl up and die.

The jacket was good though. It smelled of Dad, a rich warm scent that reminds me of nights on the couch, playing foot wars with Grea, Dad caught between us. It has the added benefit of making me feel less naked, not that I've *been* naked but there's something about the fug, about the way it covers my legs but leaves my chest bare, that inspires vulnerability.

As weird as it sounds, I'm growing used to the fug, no longer stumbling over the new toes, coming to appreciate the ability to fall distances that would have once landed me in Med.

It certainly made getting to Agriculture Three – three decks below A/Rec One – a lot faster.

Grea's here somewhere, I can feel her, the dark strands of the other curling through the rich cherry red of her presence.

Ag Three is *Citlali's* lowest deck, where all the produce from Ags One and Two is stored. The main sub-light engine bay is down here too, way up at the back. It's also where all the ship's freight tubes terminate, which makes avoiding the main Ag spaces easier. The whole way down, trepidation turns my spine in a mess of tight muscles and nerves.

I'm waiting for the Ag AI to show up, remembering her special brand of crazy, the way she was able to *emote*. The tension makes my skin crawl, and the moment I step out of the freight tubes and into the huge freight terminal, it feels like my flesh is going to waltz off my bones.

The terminal is a mess, stacked high with crates that never made it to storage, rich with the scent of rotting food. Mould, *actual* mould, spills out of the tops, oozing under lids and trailing down the plascrete sides. The one place where a hull breach might have actually done some good, flash-freezing the produce the crew needed to survive, and it looks like Ag Three has full atmosphere.

The map I stole glows above my palm, fizzing and spitting, showing the terminal as a big open space at the centre of a jumble of corridors and storage rooms.

Grea's somewhere in that maze. I could just wander around, but that'd mean more risk of running into the Ag AI, and I'd rather space myself than do that. The quickest way to find her is to use the map, but I'm having trouble deciphering the symbols.

I'm not sure if it's the map itself, or the fug interfering with my biocomp, but the holo is weird, broken and fuzzing around the edges, looking like it's been drawn by two different hands. There are symbols that spark little bits of *alien* in my brain, that make sense to the *other* but have no place within me, and then there are familiar human words, like Ag Three and Freight Station A31 with symbols my *human* brain recognises, but the *other* puzzles over, stares at.

One of the symbols *looks* like it might say "food storage" but... I don't know. I start down the nearest corridor anyway. It's dark, with just the occasional emergency glow to light my way, which is why I don't see the massive wall of fug blocking my path until I'm practically *in* it.

Sometimes, like right now, the two sides of my brain get all mixed up and I can't quite tell what I'm staring at, except that I should know what it is.

The knowledge is on the tip of my brain, hanging there, waiting for me to pick it up, but it's surrounded by fog and slippery as fuck. Frustration rises in my gut, coming out of my throat as a growl.

On my shoulder, Dude hums, saturating my brain with calming gold.

He's been doing that a lot, almost non-stop since I slid out of the bulkhead separating the crew from the rest of the ship. Guilt pools in the pit of my stomach. He's trying hard, really hard, to keep me from going all angry and I appreciate it, really I do, but right now... Right now, I just... I can't keep it in and this shit with my brain, with the words getting all jumbled up and feeling like there's this other part of me. That's shitting me off.

Shitting.

Me.

Off.

Would someone just stand up and say, 'Hey Kuma, it's all good, go back home, catch a few z's and we'll let you know when it's done'?

Or just give me a translator. Or fix my head, or... or...

Fug-rage surges from my gut, ripping out of my throat in a growl. I don't know if it's my new, deeper voice or if the fug wrapped around my throat is doing something to the sound, because Old Terra, it sounds like a rucnart in here. The bloodcurdling growl nothing Jørgen vocal cords should be able to produce.

It feels good. Powerful. Feels like I don't have to give a fuck about the look in Jim Engineer's eyes or the lies clinging to Dad. Or anything. Anything at all. Not even the massive wall of fug blocking my way.

The jumble of words is still a jumble, the meaning eluding my grasp, but that fug... It's a seething mass of grey-green sealing off the corridor, giant curling vines knotted together so tight I doubt even atmosphere can get through.

There's ash on the deck around it, scorch marks on the bulkheads, signs of someone wielding a Franken-thrower with extreme prejudice, but the wall is intact.

*Awareness* is throwing more numbers into my brain – thirteen centimetres thick, four metres wide, four tall – and for just a second, the word/symbol I was staring at gains meaning. "Danger". And for right now, I'm not sure if that's the Jørgen part of my brain or the alien one saying that.

The growl is back in my throat, lifting out of the indecision, and Dude's hum stutters, the golden fuzz faltering just long enough for the fug-rage to push it aside. 'We're going in, Dude.'

There might have been a chitter, tiny claws digging into my shipsuit, but I'm striding toward the fug-wall, pushing the fug-anger ahead of me. Grea is behind there, and nothing's going to stop me from finding her.

The wall shivers, grey-green vibrating. And for a second, I think I'm going to have to cut my way through, can already feel the fug-blades forming on the back of my hands with the thought. Then a section of the wall moves, vines writhing around each other, making a hole.

I wonder if Ag AI is through there, waiting to suck me into vacuum.

Dude chitters.

I shake the thought off. 'Yeah. Yeah. Time to get to work.'

Grea's trail leads to the back of Ag Three. The engines are around here somewhere, not the fusion drive that moves us faster-than-light – that's higher up, taking up space between the back quarter of Stasis and Engineering – these are the slower, sub-light-speed ones, the ones that move Citlali around solar systems not between them.

The fug is thick, pressing on every side of me, long strands of it choking the corridors.

It's like trying to push my way through a jungle, feet getting tangled in the roots snaking over the deck, vines forever snagging my arms and snatching at my collar. There's a sense of waiting, of tension flowing through the fug, and it's creeping down my spine, making my breath come a little shorter and my heart beat a little harder.

I'm glad for the fug over my collarbone, because Dude's the same, tiny claws kneading my shoulder. Without the armour, I'm pretty sure he'd have shredded my skin an hour ago, maybe got all the way to bone with his new talons.

The fug's tension isn't directed at me though. It slides apart, shifting and twisting, clearing as much of a path for me as it can. That's what really makes my spine crawl, wondering what it is that fug worries about more than the guy who made a habit of turning it into ash.

What scares fug? As far as I know, it's an apex predator, eating steelcrete as readily as it does flesh. Personally, the only thing I'm scared of more than fug is h'Rawd, but he can't touch the fug, can't even sense Aeotu.

I push through a final clump of fug vines, thicker than any I've encountered so far, the nanites slower to move, reluctant almost.

I pop through the vines into a... I guess you'd call it a clearing. The space beyond is clear of fug, just the *Citlali's* off-white, square-edged bulkheads, a thick, corridor-wide hatch up ahead. There's not a scratch or a scorch mark in sight, like stepping back in time to before all this started. I turn, just make sure that the fug-jungle is still there, and yeah, there it is in all its grey-green glory.

My heart picks up, dumping the first trickle of adrenalin into my system.

Because this isn't worrisome at all. Nope, no way.

The *awareness* is stirring, an uneasy churn in my gut.

There are words on the hatch, emblazoned on the surface. Not "DANGER, VACUUM", which would be icing on the shit cake, but "CAUTION, ENGINES", which you would think is better, would slow my heart a little, maybe roll back the sick feeling, but no, that would be too easy. In fact, *this* is too easy. Why is Grea in the engine room? The sense of her is thick in the air and it's coming from behind the hatch.

Sure, she likes to tinker with stuff, like the enviros in our quarters, but this... Engines are little more complicated.

I creep forward, one step, two. I'm shaking, the trickle of adrenalin flowing faster with every millimetre toward the hatch and away from the safety of the fug.

Huh. Safety. I stop, look back at it. 'Dude, when did I start to think of the fug as safe?'

He doesn't answer, doesn't even *fuzz*. In fact— He's not there, or at least it *looks* like he's not there. I can still see the tiny furrows he's digging in the fug, but I can't see him.

'Dude?'

Invisible. He's gone invisible.

Shit.

I turn back to the hatch, eyes scanning every particle. It looks just like a regular hatch, rounded corners, smooth. Just those letters painted over it.

*Deep breaths, Kuma, deep breaths.*

My hands on the hatch, pushing it open. It should creak, that's what the creepy doors do in vids, *screech* as the idiot hero enters the realm of nightmares. Of course, I've got nightmares coming out of my wazoo, so maybe I've reached my quota of *screech*es, maybe silence is all I'm going to get for the rest of my life.

I'd prefer the sound, because my imagination is creating all sorts of things worse than the ear-splitting scream of metal on metal.

The reality is… Nothing.

Clean lines of the engine room. I pad farther in, tension riding my bones, standing my hair on end, but some of the adrenalin is leeching from my system, and my heart isn't trying to break my ribs.

Dude is a different story, still invisible, still silent as the grave. It's the only thing that stops me from dropping my guard, keeps my eyes sharp and my steps light.

But still… It's nice to walk into a room and not have shit leap out at me—

Red is one of those colours that sparks a primal reaction deep in the brain, the leftover bits of *Homo sapien* from the time in our evolution where everything could kill us.

I turn a corner formed by the huge generators that make up whatever this part of the sub-light engines is, and the red is everywhere. Not a muted, muddy red either, but a bright screaming, Old-Terra-I'm-gonna-die red.

There's a bulkhead ahead of me, a big thick one. I know it's thick because there are holes in it big enough for me to crawl through, and maybe, if the holes were neat circles bored through the steelcrete, I wouldn't worry so much, but these have been eaten and the culprit is dribbling down the sides like blood.

Red fug.

Red fug throwing off the same cherry trail as my sister.

Veins of it thread through the holes, pulsing with light sharp enough to cut through my eyeballs. They pulse in a strange rhythm – *BOOM BO BO BOOM BUH* – over and over again. There's no sound, but the light... I'm getting a headache, and the ground doesn't feel as steady as it did a second ago, or maybe that's me, swaying.

*{{ Out. }}*

Yeah. Yeah, that seems like a good idea. Now, if only I can get my feet to cooperate, but there's interference somewhere between my brain and appendages. I'm having difficulty remembering where they are or how to make them move. The room tilts, the deck getting closer. Hands out, face kissing the deck, brain swimming in confusion. Trying to find my feet, to make my fingers move, to get up. And still that red pulse pounds in my eyes, echoes through my head.

*BOOM BO BO BO BOOM BUH.*

*{{ Danger. }}*

I know.

*BOOM.*

I'm trying.

*BO.*

My brain hurts.

*BO.*

I find my fingers. My hands come next.

*BOOM.*

Push off the deck.

*BUH.*

I'm on my knees, but that light's still pulsing, and now it feels like my heart, like the blood in my veins and... and...

There's a shadow, a dark rush of movement. Violence. I hear screaming, the high-pitched shriek of fug.

Something's coming at my face, a roll of red flying through the air. There's gold in my brain, Dude *fuzzing*. And then there's Dude, leaping off my shoulder, flying through the air, encased in fug armour.

More screaming.

More red, more shadows.

*BOOM.*

I'm waiting.

*BO.*

Waiting for Aeotu.

*BO.*

Waiting for the word to shiver through the air.

*BOOM.*

The one I hate.

*BUH.*

Sister.

But it doesn't come.

Instead, there's something else. A presence carried on the red rolling toward me, fighting the shadows.

I'm already half in the eter, already staring at the mess around me through a psionic veil, which is why I see it, the lightning rising above the red. As nebulous as Aeotu herself, as alien, but as familiar, as dear to me as Grea.

I twist my brain, feel the stretch as I slip through the fabric of the real and... For a nano-second I see it, a shadow in the darkness, thin and fragmented, writhing through the cherry that sings of Grea.

And then it's gone, exploding in my brain, disintegrating with a scream to rival the fug's. Shredding my ears, melting my bones.

I scream with it.

I'm face down on the deck, and somehow, some way, I'm no longer in the engine room but the corridor. It's dark, but the floor has its own glow, not bright, and if my nose wasn't pressed against it, if the corridor around me wasn't so very dark, I wouldn't have noticed.

My mouth has that old sock taste and there's a trickle of... I don't know, something, it's a trickle running from my nose, over my upper lip.

I taste it. Coppery, maybe a little salty. Blood.

Yay. Bloody nose.

I push myself up, glad that my arms work. The light from the floor casts the corridor in twilight, picking out the vines of the fug jungle and the little sentinel sitting in front of me, still in his fug armour.

Dude.

'What *was* that?'

*{{ Danger. }}*

The voice jolts, an electric current running through my nerve endings, and now that the red is no longer pounding my brain, I realise that it's new and it comes from the place in my gut where the *awareness* resides. It brings other things with it as well, a wealth of information that floods my brain and makes up seem like down and turns yellow into the taste of engine oil as it tries to find a home in my brain.

There is a *click*, a moment as the voice's information-dump overwhelms my senses, leaving me spinning in things I can't quite make out, and then calm. *Awareness* rises out of my gut, takes hold of the all the data and... orders it. It's a cool, green presence, creeping over my skin and sitting beside me in the eter, fading in and out of my perception, there and then not. A mirage on my skin.

I tilt my head again, peering at it through slitted eyes, and see... fug. The cool green thing is fug, and not just any fug, but *my* fug, the stuff turning my hands into claws and my feet in paws. That fug.

And now... now it's taking all that stuff from the voice and sorting it. A tingle runs through my nerves, gentle but insistent, and the mirage is staring at me or something, because I'm pretty sure it doesn't have eyes. And now the tingle is an unpleasant jolt and there's an expectation hovering between us.

I blink out of the eter. Then blink again. There's a screen in front of my face, lines and diagrams... and symbols I kinda, *maybe* understand, like trying to read the map except this time there's that cool green sitting next to me, making sense out of the things I'm seeing, or the non-Jøran ones at least.

Reading an ancient Terran book through wavy glass would be easier, but slowly the stuff on the screen starts to make sense.

It feels like the *awareness* knows, and instead of symbols and lines, colours spread across the screen. Vibrant, eye-searing red and a calming blue, filling in the gaps between lines. Long thin rectangles and fat curves.

I recognise a map, or the same map I was looking at on my palm unit, except this one is spread before me in some kind of heads-up display, overlaying the corridor, highlighting the edges in white, picking out the scars on the bulkheads, the fug clinging to the ceiling. Fainter white lines hug the curves of what looks like doors hidden in the bulkheads. The strange, swirling symbols pop up over each as my eyes roll over them. More information that hovers on the tip of my brain, hanging just out of reach.

I guess it's Aeotu's language. Whatever that is.

The meaning of the red is pretty clear though, especially when I roll over a patch of the red fug. There's no scream, but the display flashes and throbs, stabbing my eyes.

I jerk away, eyes streaming.

'Stop! Message received. Red is bad.'

The cool green in my head pulses. There's no emotion attached, just a pulse, an acknowledgement.

Dude hops onto my knee, humming away.

The fug armour makes him look even more like a miniature rucnart, sleeking out all the fuzz, making his muzzle sharper, his legs longer. He's even got a tail now – as long as he is and tipped with a wicked barb. His ears though... His ears are *huge* – satellites attached to his tiny head, twitching and turning with a life of their own.

Satisfaction rolls off of him.

'Choose that yourself?'

He hums. I think that's a yes.

So, what was the red stuff and why does it feel like Grea? I remember it from before, following Core/drone through the ruined remnants of Stasis deck. The stuff had wound in with the other fug, red like blood, dripping from the holes in the stasis units, clinging to the bulkheads. It hadn't noticed me then, not like it was now, and I can't help but think Grea has something to do with it.

The *awareness* is urging me to turn back, to find the safety of A/Rec. I can feel the cool green in the back of my head. I ignore it. Grea is here somewhere, in the mess of Aeotu and *Citlali*. I feel her like she's standing beside me, watching, waiting. Being absolutely no use at all except as a lodestone, a game of hot or cold, where my only clue to her location is the strength with which she glares at me.

I can't go back.

I turn to stare at the engine room hatch.

I have to find my sister.

# CHAPTER TEN

Trying to force my way back into the engine room is an exercise in futility. As soon as I get within three paces of the hatch, the fug jungle is on me like a bad case of stink. Wrapping around my arms and waist, holding me back while it crawls all over the Citlali's once-white bulkheads. Eventually, there's a half-metre of grey-green nano-tech between me and the engine room's hatch.

I'd accuse it of being Grea, or Grea of being it, getting between me and where I want to go just to piss me off. Except I can feel Grea, and she's not in the grey-green.

Instead, I go up. And up, and up, following that trail of Grea, crawling through maintenance tubes, fug-feet slipping on ladder rungs, for once more nuisance than help. I go all the way past the Ag decks, and both A/Recs, sticking close to the back of the ship and the engines, and I keep climbing until I'm back where all this started.

Stasis.

I shiver as I crawl out of the access hatch. Ghosts haunt the deck. I feel them on my neck, knowing without having to look that there are more bodies lying here than there are walking around. That gem comes from the *awareness;* an exact count hovers on the tip of my consciousness, there if I want to reach for it. I don't.

Not all of them are dead, and not all of the bodies are here, the *awareness* shares that too, although I remember it on my own well enough; the minds reaching out to me in the dark place where Aeotu changed me.

Yeah, I remember a lot of things. Like how, before I was ejected into space, the engine containment was failing, how the miniature sun that powered the faster-than-light drive was going to explode and turn us all into atoms. I remember, too, standing in the corridor on A/Rec listening to Jim Engineer say he'd fixed the shielding but didn't have the material to kickstart the fusion generator.

So, point one: I'm clearly not dead, which means the reactor didn't blow, and point two: someone must have found some fusion material 'cause that sucker was *on*. And last but not least, I'm almost half-sure that Jim wasn't the one to plaster the reactor core with red fug.

The bulkhead at the back of the little Engineering lab is gone, as are the walls of the maintenance tunnel behind it, and the freight tube beyond *that*, leaving a straight shot to the main engine.

The miniature sun is no longer the dull orange of a dying star, it blazes bright enough to burn out my retinas. Only the shimmer of the containment field and the fug combine to refract the light and save my eyes. I'm not so sure about the rest of me though.

It's bad. Really, really bad. The red fug is crawling all over the reactor, cords of energy writhing over it, curling around each individual strand as if to cage the power. Heat rises off of the core, a haze warping the air, bringing with it the scent of burnt ozone and the acrid, musty taste of ash.

The sense of Grea is strongest here, feels like she's standing right beside me; but she's not. She's in *there* somewhere, behind the writhing wall of red. Behind the containment field, as impossible as that is. If Grea is behind the containment field, then she's burning alive.

She's my twin; I'd feel that, *know* that. All I feel, all I know is that Grea is *here* but not.

'Grea!' *Grea!* I yell her name with voice and mind.

The red shivers.

'Grea!' *Grea!*

The red moves, vines separating from the wall, turning like

they're looking at me, and for a moment there's a presence, an intelligence staring back at me.

'Grea?'

It rumbles, a deep, steady GRUUMMMM.

I step forward. Dude huddles against my neck. 'Grea, are you there? Can you hear me?'

GRUUMMM.

Another step, but while my feet are moving forward, I can't help the part of me that leans back, that whispers that this isn't right. 'Just hang on, I'm going to get you out—'

A red spear hurtles at my face.

I throw myself aside, feeling the burn of the fug weapon on my back.

*{{ Danger. }}*

'I know! Tell me something useful!'

There's no response, but the voice is growing stronger, rising behind the cool green of the fug. I can see it, not just on the eter, but *see* it, with my eyes, floating around me like fog, rising out of the deck, taking on form beside me.

It looks like the *Citlali* AI, and yet… not. Different. It's faceless, with but the suggestion of features, a squished nose, the vague shape of too-big eyes. It opens a slash that might be a mouth, showing protrusions that might be canines – too long and too sharp to be human, too small to be kin. And somehow, some way, it's linked to Hunt.

When it speaks, it uses Core's voice. *{{ Run, Kuma. }}*

'Core?'

It shakes its head. *{{ No. Run. }}*

'No, I have to find Grea.'

*{{ Not here. }}*

'Then where?'

*{{ Not here. Run. }}*

No. No.

Grea is *here*, I can feel her. Somewhere amongst the mess of fug and the crumbled remnants of Stasis, my sister is waiting for me, drawing me on.

*{{ Run! }}*

I run; I run straight into the fug.

The fug armour responds. One second I'm me, all fleshy and pale gold, the next I'm sheathed in grey-green, plates interlocking over my arms, clicking into place over my face, the weird visor thing over my eyes. And then there are blades coming out of my arms and there's red all around me, screaming in my ears, smacking against my ribs, my back, reaching for legs and feet. *Slash, slash, slash.* My arms know what to do without me telling them, and tendrils of the red stuff crash to the deck, severed sections of vines wailing a new song, one of rage and pain.

And still the red fug fights, a new vine thunking into my sides for every one I cut down. *THUNK THUNK THUNK.* There's no pain. No crushing, crunching snap. Just the hollow sound as they beat against my armour. The sound reverberates in my bones

Through it all, I can feel Grea sitting on the edge of my awareness, there and yet not.

Heat. It starts out as a small discomfort against my back, another pain amidst the dozen sneaking through the armour. It's nothing, and then it's everything, consuming my spine, racing over my scalp, clutching my cheekbones in molten talons and going for my eyes.

An inferno ripping through my skin,

I scream, but there's no air, no sound, nothing save the fire.

Red is taking over my vision, flashing and wailing, and there's that voice, Core/not-Core yelling at me, her/its words a jumble of lip movements and arms. I can't hear her/it, can't hear anything but the rush of flame.

I'm on the deck, and there's the red fug, eating through the grey-green stuff, turning it to ash, just like it's turning me to ash, eating my armour, seeking out the flesh beneath.

No.

No.

I roll. Thrash. My hands are blocks of steelcrete, numb and clumsy, resisting my brain. I roll again, slapping useless limbs on the deck, against my sides, trying to reach the molten hole at the base of my spine, needing to reach it, to rip it off and—

There's a shape above me. Huge. Dark. Blocking out the slashing tendrils of fug. And then it's gone, leaping over me into the arms of the red.

I'm twisting, knees under me, pushing off the deck. Watching. Blades the length of my arms rip at the vines, making them screech and wail.

Alarms blare in front of my face, screaming red, like the fug, and Core/not-Core wails in my ear. I'm spinning around, blades springing from my own arms. Hunt films my vision, makes my heart loud and sluggish, slows down time until I'm moving through seconds like they're minutes. Long, dragging strings of time in which to twist and cut. The fug's wail becomes a song of pain, tendrils hitting the deck, turning to dust. There's a warm spot in the small of my back, a sense of the other – saviour, person, helper – moving, of their presence, perceived not by my empathy, but on the tingle of the *awareness*. I move and he moves, each of us spinning and slashing like we're two parts of a whole. Breathing together, hearts beating in unison.

Hunt, or something like it, is riding him too, and with the bit of my brain that is still me, the piece hidden behind Hunt, I wonder if this is how the tree-kin feel, what it's like to be part of a pack, the sense that I'm not alone.

A brother/not-brother watching my back.

It's not like what I have with Grea, there's none of the friction, the constant nagging, the fighting, even amongst the closeness of twins. Without thinking, he's at my side, and we're hacking and slashing in unison, Hunt silent in my head but the map over my face updating, showing us the way forward.

Aeotu floats between Mac and I, a conduit negating the need for speech or thought.

I lose time, lose everything but the wail of fug and the endless swing of my blades, the way they slice through tendril after tendril. It's hypnotic.

My arms ache, and there's a pit of hunger eating through my belly when we stop.

One moment I'm a cog in a two-part wrecking machine, and the next I'm... not. Aeotu is gone as easily as she came, the connection to my not-brother with it, and I'm alone in my brain, without even the *awareness* for company. I'm hot, my breath is coming hard, and the deck looks really, really good right now, comfy almost.

A hand grips my arm before my knees melt.

There're no words, but that connection is back, running through my armour, hitting my brain. Warm and bloodthirsty, single-minded. But behind Aeotu, I sense something else, a familiar orange, a dull throb of emotion. Calm but not.

'Mac?'

There's no response, just that hand on my arm, tugging me up and forward.

I tug back, grabbing the other by the shoulders and spinning him around. He's humanoid, that much I can tell through the grey-green of his fug armour, but everything else... The Mac from the eter. His faceplate a solid shield, featureless, shiny, a little too long for a human face, a little too narrow. And his shoulders... The Mac I remember is tall and not big, not muscled up but he actually used the gym, had muscles like solid bits of rope in his arms. The Mac before me is huge, a rucnart taken to its hind legs. And maybe it is, maybe that familiar orange tickling the back of my eter is wishful thinking, a ghost of my best friend's anima somehow clinging to the thing in front of me.

'Mac?' I say again.

A response, so tiny, so faint it could be a trick of my imagination. A flash of something on the very edge of psionic reach.

I dive in, leaving my body behind, trusting it to Dude and the fug armour to protect me. The last bit feels wrong, dangerous in a way that I shouldn't even contemplate, but... Is this Mac? I'm in my eter before I've even really thought it through. Mac would do the same for me if he could. I know he would, deep down in the pit of me. He's a part of me in the same way that Grea is a part of me, connected to my anima by the bonds of friendship and the start of something deeper, he just does his best to ignore it.

Threads of the fug's grey-green still wind through the psionic plane, still creep around me, forming their mirage over my skin though my fug parts are more solid, lacing over my feet and winding up my arms, still ghostly but... I don't know. More a part of me, taking on the vibrant pink-red of my being. They feel different too, still alien, still aware but... Complex and... agreeing, or is that promising? Whatever it is, there's the sense of protection of... looking after my body, standing in the corridor.

Okay. That's new.

The glimmer is on the edge of the eter, and I have no time to contemplate the latest development. Pale orange, a ripple of silver within a casing of bronze.

I reach for it, leaving the fug behind, even the fug-me. For the first time since I came out of the stasis unit, I'm just me, and it feels... lonely and free and... There's no time for this. The orange flash that's Mac, fades. Or maybe it runs, it's hard to tell. He's a mirage, eluding me even as I chase him, never getting closer, but not getting any farther away either.

*Mac.* I push the thought ahead of me, encasing it in a complex wave of emotion. Patience, anticipation, happiness, welcome. The warmth of home, of old memories, of the tight knot in the pit of my anima, the bit he gave me that's more than the affection of friends. The bit he pretends he forgot. There's no colour to describe the emote, it just is. It's a Mac-seeking missile and it arrows after that glimmer faster than he can possibly escape—

I feel it hit him, a shudder in the fabric of the eter, a tug on the knot in my chest. Feel him stop, feel...

Feel Aeotu. Cold and sharp, the kaleidoscope of her being no longer a conduit between us but a web under his skin.

I stop.

Aeotu/Mac stops.

Turns.

I'm in front them/him. Staring up at that face, the dark brows, the square chin, seeing through it like his flesh is crystal and underneath...

A flat nose and liquid eyes every colour of the rainbow stares back at me. Double arms squished under Mac's skin, wrapped around his torso, whorls and lines carved into stone-like skin, twisting and turning, capturing my gaze, drawing me in.

'Aeotu.'

*Sister.*

'Get out of him.'

Refusal, it shines violet from under Mac's skin.

I feel the flesh peel back from my teeth, feel the prick as they sharpen, feel my ankles bend and my fingers ache and lengthen. Feel the vines of fug-me, crawling up my legs, wrapping solid, grey-pink tendrils around my calves.

Aeotu/Mac shrinks.

A growl rumbles through the eter, shaking the endless white, even as rage gleams red at my feet.

I lunge. Arms wrap around Aeotu/Mac, grey-pink encasing them/him in vines and dive into their being, trying to peel back the layers of Aeotu and—

Aeotu is gone, vanished without a fight, leaving just me and Mac in the eter.

'Kuma?'

'Mac.' I step back, feel the smile break my face even as relief saturates the air. 'Hey.'

Confusion rides the space between his eyes, knotting the skin together and rising around him in a muddy grey fog. He looks down, at the Mac-fug gathered around his feet and hands. The first spark of alarm turns the confusion green.

'It's just fug.' I step forward, dipping down a little to catch his eyes. 'It's okay, I've got it too. See?' I lift my hands, twisting and turning them to show off the ghost of claws hovering around my fingers. A little concentration and a twitch of my forearm and the blades spring out too. 'Just fug,' I say again, keeping the smile on my face. Or trying to.

It's kinda hard when Mac's just looking at me, brows still crunched together and those bright sparks of alarm running through his emotions.

I'm waiting for him to say something. Anything. My name was a good start. But he just continues to stare.

'Mac?'

Nothing. Well, almost nothing. His eyes are moving, drifting over my face, finally looking at my hands. He reaches out, traces a finger over the fug-me, starting in the palm of my hand and then up, over my wrist, the inside of my arm, leaving a tingle in his wake, a fine, heady fuzz that spreads through my skin and makes my toes want to curl. He keeps tracing, over my shoulder, across my collarbone. It takes me longer than it should, a second that feels like a minute...

I'm blaming it on the tingle, on half-filled wishes and dreams I haven't told anyone about. It's not until Mac's finger finishes tracing across my chest and over my opposite shoulder that I realise, he's not touching *me*. I mean, he kind of is, because you know... Whatever. The thing that has Mac's attention isn't me, it's just *on* me, or in me or... you know what, I'll sort it out later. Right now, the important thing is that my best friend is concentrating on the air next to my left ear. Concentrating really, *really* hard, and that knot of confusion between his brow... it's changing, the lines deepening, the bewildered, slightly blank expression turning hot and angry, the air around him boiling.

Literally. Boiling.

I'm halfway across the eter, a good rucnart length between us. The movement isn't... mine I know that deep in the pit of myself. I'm stilling going *what the fuck?*, staring at Mac through the haze of superheated air, twisting my brain around the change in his emotions, in the firestorm of red and black snaking around his legs.

Mac stalks after me. The eter shakes with every step, fissures opening up the ground, shooting toward me, seeking me out, pushing a new gravity before it, trying to suck me into the pool of rage beneath.

And I'm away again, an ocean between me and Mac, between me and the rage surrounding him. And again, I wasn't the one who moved. Whatever it was, it came from *outside*, but still... but still a part of me. Mac's coming at me, the rage storm getting bigger, swallowing, stretching across the eter with those fissures of rage, but far enough away for me to breathe, to wonder, to slowly, oh so slowly, turn my head and look at the air next to my ear. There's a loadstone in my gut, a weight of dread and the first blooming of denial pulling me down.

It's like trying to see in the dark, trying to pick out shapes your eyes aren't equipped to see. I catch a shimmer out the corner of my eye, but when I turn to face it, tucking in my chin and twisting my neck muscles until they scream, it's gone. I spin, trying to catch a glimpse of the thing. Spin, spin, spin.

For a crazy moment, I'm an Old Terran dog chasing its tail in circles, trying to catch the impossible. Then there are hands on my shoulders, burning hands, catching me, lifting me up, caging me in molten rage. I brace for pain, for the shearing, fatty stench of burning flesh, for fire to race across my face. It doesn't come, not like I expect.

There's pain, ripping across my chest, razor blades scoring the inside of my flesh, all the way down my arm to the palm of my hand. There's blood from my mouth, from the tips of my fingers, from my nose. I'm screaming and choking at the same time, trying to drag air into my lungs, trying to expel the fountain of pain.

And then it's done. Gone. Not even an echo left behind. Just... me, Mac, and the bloody, wriggly golden thing in his hand.

'Dude?'

Mac's face is a snarl, his teeth rucnart-long, his whole face distorting, his fist growing claws, piercing Dude, crushing the critter in his fist—

'No!' Fear bursts before me, a semi-focused wave of emotion blasting through Mac's hand, freeing Dude.

The critter tumbles, and then he's in *my* hand. This time I move, blasting through Mac's cage, shredding the bars before Mac has a chance to blink.

And now Mac is snarling at me.

Okay. Enough of this shit.

Pro tip, never piss off an empath.

I slap Mac down. A wave of anger and he's immobile.

He struggles, but slowly sanity seeps back into his eyes, enough for him to glare at me. 'Let me go, Kuma.'

'No.'

Fear wraps around him, chases some of the anger from his face. 'You gotta let me go. You *have* to.'

'Why?'

He doesn't say anything, but there's a look, a quick glance at the air next to his ear, and a spike of something deeper than fear. Terror.

I follow his gaze and see... nothing. Just empty air.

And still, dread curls around my feet.

Against my chest, Dude fuzzes, not an ordinary fuzz, not trying to comfort or inspire. It's different, silver instead of gold, reaching up through my bones, wrapping around my eyes and twisting. The space next to Mac's ear shimmers, that mirage from before. I squint. The shimmer is stubborn, like not in the way a lock is stubborn, but in the way Grea is stubborn, an active *don't bother me fathead* kind of stubborn, twisting and turning, *pushing* at me, telling me to go away, to look elsewhere.

I focus harder.

The shimmer gives way with a *pop*, a burst of light and colour strong enough to force me back a step.

And there it is. There. It. Is.

The fuzzy, fuggy thing sitting on Mac's shoulder looks like a critter, like Dude, but not; grey-green where Dude is gold, a twisting, shifting rainbow at its claws and threaded through its coat. The rainbow curls through Mac's skin, sinking into his marrow, spreading through bone and muscle in a fine web. Wrapping around his brain stem, controlling him. I move to rip it out—

*Mac* shoves me away. Not the rainbow stuff, not the fuggy critter-like thing on his shoulder. Mac. The bronze of his determination trails through the eter, leaves imprints on my chest.

'No, Kuma.' His voice rumbles, deeper than before, an edge of metal underlying the natural timbre. 'I need it. It's helping me.'

'It's controlling you.'

'Maybe, but it's better than the alternative.' He looks down.

And that's when I see it, the red at Mac's feet isn't just rage. It churns with the same lightning the red fug does, crawling up his legs, trying to slip under his skin. Except the rainbow is there, a glowing shield beating it back.

Aeotu at war with the same presence that's wound up in my sister.

My grip on Mac loosens.

He's gone.

I stand there, staring at the endless white of the empty eter. Little by little, slow enough that I don't notice it at first, fug-me seeps through the white, turns the eter into a forest of pink and grey. It wraps around me, claiming my feet, my hands, crawling up my back.

It whispers and the sound feels like home.

# CHAPTER ELEVEN

I blinked back into the real to find just me and Dude standing in that corridor. Alone. Not even a farewell or a boot print to let me know that Mac had been there.

Nothing.

I hot-footed it out of there, heading up another deck to Engineering, trying to find another way to Grea, wherever Aeotu had stashed her. And why? Why had Aeotu taken Grea from the family stasis unit? Hidden her?

It didn't make sense, not a lick.

All the usual routes to Engineering where cut off, thick with fug walls where the corridors weren't collapsed altogether, even the way I came. I didn't try cutting through, not when I saw the red stuff threaded through the grey-green. Not after the last time.

After what felt like forever of crawling through access tubes and the spaces between decks, of cutting my way through bulkheads and dropping down decks only to go back up, I stopped following the readout on my visor – the HUD. The red fug was everywhere, igniting warnings, making the HUD scream and Dude growl when I got too close. There was no way up, not from the inside at least.

So now I'm on *Citlali's* outer ring, staring at an airlock. It's not the usual kind of airlock, not the really big ones for shuttles or people. It's hidden in its own little closet, shielded by thick walls and a hatch that doesn't have a name, just a number engraved in the steelcrete. Discrete, invisible almost. It's one of those doors you're not meant to notice unless you need it, just another part of the bulkhead. The kind Jim Engineer used to grumble about, 'cause he always missed the damn thing, even with his biocomp showing him the way.

It's the kind with a genetic lock, one of those we never even mucked around with as kids, not after the first time at least. Every intrusion was sent straight to Captain Lyn, and she would make you wish it was h'Rawd's teeth you were staring down. She wouldn't yell, just stand there, straight and proud, looking down her nose in that way that made you want to sink into the decking and never come out. Even if you didn't remember a word she said, you remembered that look, the one that said you did wrong and if you ever did it again she'd flush you out of that airlock and not feel a twinge of remorse. I used to wonder if she learnt the trick from Mwat.

Now, I just remember the captain's hand reaching out of mouldy stasis gel, the stench of decomposition ripe in the air, and throwing up until there was nothing left in my stomach. I hold the memory, letting it play behind my eyes as I slice through the lock with my fug blades. They sink into the steelcrete without a sound. There's resistance, just a little, and I push harder, push until my knuckles kiss the hatch, before angling down. The hatch is thick, thicker than I expected, but then I guess it's a hole in the protective shell of the *Citlali*. A punch in the membrane that keeps us safe from the vacuum of space. So yeah, I guess it should be thick. Slicing down is harder than slicing through, and I have to use every bit of strength and most of my weight to force the fug blades down. There's an extra bit of resistance, a moment where all movement stops just long enough for me to wonder if perhaps I've found something fug blades can't defeat, before I'm moving again. I guess those were the bolts holding the hatch in place.

Then it's done. The lock is nothing more than shredded steelcrete, and I'm pushing it open.

There's no light beyond, just darkness and cold. The HUD flashes and now I'm picking out the lines of another hatch and another lock in faint shades of green; so faint I'm squinting. Apparently, even the dark of the airlock is too dark for fug-vision, because light floods the area from a new glow on my shoulder.

And crap, is it cold. Freezing. I'm shivering even through my layer of fug-armour.

I push the inner door closed behind me and spend a few moments wondering how I'm going to get it to stay that way, now that I've shredded the bolts meant to keep it shut. The answer's in the fug, because, you know, why wouldn't it be?

As I'm running my hands over the hatch, a finger-length of my amour detaches and slips into the gap between door and bulkhead. I don't know exactly what it's doing, but the *awareness* tells me it's fixing the bolts.

Huh. Cool.

Slicing through the outer airlock is as bad as the first, worse maybe, because the cold makes my muscles clench, shivering to keep warm. Keeping the blades steady is becoming a challenge with the way my hands shake.

It would be really great if the fug-armour had heating. I'm thinking that, of being toasty warm and not shivering my arse off, trying to beat back the cold by imagining heat sinking into my skin, all the way through to my bones, when acknowledgement blooms from that place in the back of my head. The HUD flashes, a triangle bisected by a spiral appearing front and centre, and heat hits my skin.

'Holy Terra.' The shock of it is enough to turn my muscles liquid and make my hands shake even more. I'm barely able to keep my knees from becoming jelly, let alone keep the blades steady.

They wobble and, for a second, I think I'm in danger of cutting off my leg but then the fug-armour takes over. Joints harden, holding me up, keeping the blades in place, and for a moment, as all that happens, the golden veins under my skin, the ones Mac ripped out of my chest, blaze. And there, glowing in the corner of my eye, is Dude, sitting like a grey-green sentinel on my shoulder. Concentration rolls off him in waves.

He chitters at me.

'Fuck.' Mac was right. I don't... Something hard and sharp is digging claws into my gut. I don't want to call it fear, don't want to think that Dude is a threat because... well, because it's *Dude*.

I breathe deep. *Now's not the time, Kuma*. I have a mission, a purpose. I gotta get to Grea. And it's *Dude*, the little fuzz-ball who saved my arse, who fought fug for me. *Dude*.

I push the stuffing back into my knees, firm my muscles and as soon as I do, I feel the golden threads retreat, sense Dude relax on my shoulder.

I focus on the hatch, on forcing the blades through the steelcrete. Fear still curls in my gut adding to the vomit-inducing roil of emotion already there. There's a whole freak-out going on in the depths of my being, but I'm ignoring it. Totally. Ignoring. It.

It's going real well.

It helps that I'm not shaking my arse off. Good to know the fug-armour has climate control, 'cause it's going to get colder once I open the hatch.

The blades pop through the lock, and now I'm stepping back, eyeing the envirosuits, which, frankly, I should have thought of *before* I started cutting through the hull, but hey, better late than never right?

I should be reaching for one of the thin, nano-fibre suits on their little nooks, shoving feet and arms into it, but... I've seen fug in space, seen it moving. The armour's even keeping me warm, and I wonder...

'Fug? We're going EVA.'

EVA being short for "Everything Fucking Wants to Kill You in Vacuum". I feel... stupid. Even traitorous for talking to fug, for wanting it to do stuff for me when it's killed so many people I know, friends, not-so-much-friends. Critters. Even Core. And yet... I have fug-feet, and the armour's kept my safe so far. So... yeah.

Nothing happens at first, and that stupid feeling is growing because it's *fug* for crap's sake, but still. Of course, it probably doesn't understand English. I imagine what it's like beyond the hatch, cold and dark, no atmosphere, no pressure. The *awareness* hums. The little bit of success spurs me on, and I imagine what would happen if I stepped through without protection. I've never seen it, not even in training vids, just been told. There's no pressure in the ice hull, all the liquid in my body would flash boil, molecules expanding, and then in the seconds it took my atoms to lose all their energy, I would freeze. Freeze right down through the bone. Flesh. Blood. Hair. One giant Kuma-popsicle. Dead before the last of the oxygen had a chance to leave my lungs.

That spark of acknowledgement flares in the place beyond me, and something... shifts.

The armour changes colour, the green leeching out of the grey until all that's left is a matt steel. The plates over my arms flatten, smooth out, while new patterns coat my chest. There's a pulling at my feet, and when I look down, the turned-back ankles and paws are melting as fug moves up my legs, trailing around the back of my knees. I try to twist, to follow the migration, and get a glimpse of the armour flowing over my back. Even my HUD changes, new readouts popping to life. New symbols.

I lift my feet, one at a time, feeling the distinct *shhunck shhunk* of mag boots.

On my shoulder, Dude's armour has changed as well, and I wonder if I look as sleek as he does, aerodynamic almost.

I wonder what that's about, 'cause, you know, vacuum and aerodynamics being mutually exclusive and all that.

Still, looks like my message got through.

Meet the new Kuma, all kitted out for EVA.

Hoo-boy.

Another breath.

I'm really going to do this.

Trust fug.

I'm pushing the hatch open before I think about it.

Alarms should be squealing right about now, 'Danger, vacuum' blaring in my ears. Core yelling at me.

But only vacuum and the endless darkness of the ice hull greet me.

★

The plan is not going to plan.

The plan was to find another way to Engineering through the ice hull, to use the maintenance tubes and cut my way through the bulkhead, thereby getting around all the internal damage. It never really occurred to me there'd be external damage as well.

I'm staring at another collapsed tube, chunks of ice and splintered steelcrete blocking my way.

The maintenance tubes aren't that big to begin with, large enough for human and a hover-sled to move through without bending in half. The tubes themselves are made of thin, transparent plasglas with just enough metal in them for my mag boots to function and ribs of thick steelcrete for support.

So far, I've only brained myself on three ribs, just enough to rattle my mind and to recognise the HUD's proximity sensors.

Outside the tubes is the ice hull, which is just what it sounds like. Ice. Thirty-three metres of ink-black frozen water surround the inner hull, forming a protective layer around the habitual parts of the ship. Beyond it, the outer hull is our last line of defence, the same defences Aeotu's grappling cables punched through like brittle plasform.

The aftermath of which is what I'm looking at now.

There's a massive cable amongst the mess of ice and plasglas, silver-grey and pulsing like a muscle, veins of grey-green curling around it. Fug is everywhere, a carpet covering floor and walls, seeping through cracks in the tube and branching out into the ice. I don't know what it's doing, other than making the place look like a jungle, waving streamers in the air. For the most part, the fug is inert, not dull, lifeless inert just not doing anything. Laying there. It doesn't even react when I step on it. I wonder how much of that is because of the fug-armour, and how much is because I'm not toting a Franken-thrower and the extreme desire to use it. I mean, that desire is there but just not as... extreme as it was.

A small part of me, the part that ran around *Citlali* trying to save it, to save *us*, the part that floated in a stasis unit, is freaking out about that, wants to question everything, is scared shitless that I'm losing myself to the new parts of me, that I'm *accepting* it so easily. I mean, this shit tried to kill me once, ate people I knew, tore them up and used their parts to repair itself. Is it still doing that? Still eating corpses and critters and crew? Still tearing my home to pieces in an effort to save itself?

That part of me is a gibbering mess, spewing uncertainty and guilt like acid in my heart, making me doubt every step, every moment, every action. The other part of me, he's pushed all that shit aside.

There's no time. I have to save Grea, and I'll use anything I can get my hands on to do it. Even fug

The collapsed tube is going to be a problem. There isn't a way around it, no crawl spaces or access points, just the long, smooth line running through the ice hull. Even if I shifted the debris, I'd still have to get past the grappling cable, and that sucker is huge. Three rucnart-lengths wide and, as far as I knew, a solid ribbon of whatever the fuck it was that made up Aeotu's hull. I remembered cutting through it with the Franken-laser, remembered the scream knocking me on my arse, ringing in my ears. Remembered, too, the cable's pulse, how Aeotu seemed to peer through it and *speak* to me, the sibilant "sister" shivering through my comms.

She's not speaking to me now though, and I'm thankful for small mercies.

If I can't get through the cable, I guess the only way is around.

I study the ice beyond the maintenance tube.

At least it can't get any colder.

✶

Pummelling through ice is both easier and harder than I expected.

Easier because... well, the fug blades. And harder because the hull goes on *forever*. Well, that's what it feels like with my lungs burning for oxygen and my muscles doing their best impression of jelly. I'm sitting with my back against one side of the little tunnel I've made, sweat running over my top lip, wondering if the fug-armour can purify it so I can get rid of the crappy, glue-like taste on the back of my tongue and the desperate need for water. Yeah, that'd be real convenient. Not sure how I'd feel about it if I had to pee and it recycled *that* as well, but... yeah, let's not go there. Gross factor plus.

It's kinda ironic that I'm surrounded by enough water to drown the Ag decks three times over, and I'm sitting here, dying of thirst, or what feels like dying. At least I'm not suffocating. That would suck.

I'd made it around the blockage in the maintenance tube, slashing and hacking my way through the ice, slicing into the plasglas on the other side. I'd thought I was home clear, just a couple hundred metres to the next junction, up a level and I would be right outside Engineering, hacking through the next maintenance hatch and I'd be done.

I should be so lucky.

It hadn't been a grappling cable that blocked my way. It was the red stuff. Fug the colour of blood, writhing and pulsing like I'd expected the cable to, burning its way through the ice. My HUD screamed, that *awareness* in the pit of me yelling danger, even as Dude had snarled, coming to attention, every fibre in his little body ready to leap at the red-fug and tear it to pieces. I'd barely caught him before he kamikazed off my shoulder. And then I'd turned tail and run.

I'd thought I was running back the way I'd come, my feet seemed to know where they were going and that had been enough for me as the red-fug snapped and burned in my wake.

The stuff was everywhere, keeping pace, nipping at my heels. Hungry, angry and vengeful. It pushed the emotions ahead of it, just like Mac had in the eter, and I'd wondered, in the space between ragged breaths, if it was *him* chasing me, causing this. It was just a second, and then I'd thrown it aside because as much as the rage felt like Mac, it wasn't him. There'd been something else in the emotions chasing me, a different vibration. Similar but not the same.

Whatever drove the red-fug, it wasn't Mac and it wasn't Aeotu.

I hadn't run for long, a few minutes maybe, enough to never want to do it again. At some point, after I'd scrambled up a ladder I hadn't remembered coming down, I'd lost the red-fug. Lost the sense of it wanting to tear me apart and feast on my blood.

So now I'm sitting here, my back against the tube, dying of thirst. Sitting here and wondering where the fuck I am, 'cause I ain't anywhere near Engineering. I think I'm somewhere *near* Engineering, but... yeah. There should be a junction around here, a crosshatch of tubes, one going around the ship, just like this, the other driving straight to the inner bulkhead. That's what the map on my biocomp says, the one that shows *Citlali* as she was before. I guess Aeotu's done some remodelling, or I'm lost. Seems like my feet didn't know where they were going after all.

It could be worse, I guess. I could be floating in the void, untethered and drifting.

So yeah, there's that.

Dude doesn't seem too worried. He's scampering around the tunnel, up it, over it, his little fug-claws sinking into the ice. He's right over my head, hanging from the ceiling like the little bit of gravity that makes it into the tubes isn't there at all. He's got his nose to the... I was going to say ground, but I guess it's the roof. Whatever. He's got his nose stuck to it, passing back and forth, back and forth, scenting the plasglas like some kinda sterdane, and there's this halo of concentration around him. A bright, pulsing bronze, and I'm looking at it not with my psionic ability, but with my eyes. My. Eyes.

I guess there's only so much freakage a body can take, 'cause I'm like, just chilling here, staring at Dude and trying to figure out how long this shit has been going on. I figure it's got something to do with the fug, or the fug-HUD opening up a different spectrum of light or some such shit. All I know, all I really care about right now is that Dude's on some kinda mission. There's purpose in the halo, a thread of bronze covering his itty-bitty muzzle, wrapped around his paws. There's something else too, a shimmer seen from the corner of my eye.

I slip into the eter, not all the way, just enough to bring the shimmer into sharp focus overlaying it with what my physical eyes perceive. The colours are brighter, more vibrant, pulsing like blood. And there's the shimmer.

A chill runs through my blood, not a deluge, just a trickle. I already knew what I'd find, was just hoping I was wrong.

The same multi-hued thread that ran through Mac, connecting him to the fug-critter, sparkles along Dude's spine, all the way from his nose to the barb of his tail. It trails into the eter before disappearing, slipping through the threads of the psionic plane and into... something.

I know where it's going, the ora. Dude and Mac are talking to Aeotu, *connected* to her.

Everything's connected to her now. I guess there wasn't any real escaping that, not with her claws in *Citlali*, with fug, no matter its colour, seeping through the bulkheads, into me.

I step *away* from myself, fully into the eter, and turn. It's weird, looking at myself this way, at my body propped up against the wall, one leg up, one leg thrust out across the tube. There's a disconnect, a gap between my perception of myself and the reality. It's like looking at yourself in a mirror, you and yet not you, like looking at a fragment of yourself, an alternate being.

The boy in the tube is taller than I expected, with broader shoulders and bigger hands. I wonder how much of that is the armour and how much is me, the changes wrought between Core pushing me into that stasis unit and waking up. Patterns move across my chest, over my thighs, swirls and shapes forming and reforming on the armour's surface.

But I'm not here to admire myself in fug, as awesome and gross as that is. There's a kind of *shift* I did when I first sought Aeotu in the ship's AI core. I twist and pop, like standing on my head while doing a cartwheel. It's a change of perception, of slipping through what I *know* is reality and finding a new one, one where colours I never knew existed explode in my head. There's no describing them because I'm not even sure I'm *seeing* them. It's taste and sound and the brush of colour against my face. It's a place where nothing and everything exist all at once, a place of possibility, of making. Of darkness.

And there, there is the golden thread strung between Dude and I, the veins of him running under my skin, and under that, *in* the fug, is the rainbow. A spiderweb of every human colour and all of the impossible ones, all over me. I follow it down through my toes, into the fabric of the ora, and turn. And turn, and turn and turn. Every turn takes me deeper into the nothing, still following that thread, racing into the darkness and there, there...

Holy Terra.

# CHAPTER TWELVE

I expected the Aeotu. I expected a supernova of light and sound. I expected the shivering, alien voice reaching out. I expected "sister".

I didn't expect this.

It's not Aeotu. It's... more? Less?

It's me. Or not me. Or a twin, if a twin was an alien. Or...

I just... I can't.

The thing before me is humanoid. Four arms, two legs. A head. Skin that's not skin, but the strange alien metal-stone that forms Aeotu's bulkheads, and blood that's not formed of haemoglobin and iron, but energy, pure, blinding energy, the kind that burns organics alive. The kind that powers FTL engines. And it's not alive. Not alive like *I'm* alive or Aeotu is alive. And it's not dead either, not a tank of biogel and circuits.

It looks like me, or like the me that's slumped in the maintenance tube, covered in fug armour. The same broad chest and muscled thighs, the same pattern of lines and whorls tracing under its skin. It's... disturbing and also... I want to say cool but it doesn't feel right, not for something like this. Is it real? Does this thing *exist* or is this just a figment of my imagination? An illusion created by Aeotu?

A mirage plays around it, half-seen. Of cables and ribs, a frame holding it upright, and little spots of yellow, like heat signatures. I peer closer, trying to make out the scurrying things... they're tiny, minute. Dude is a giant beside them. I lean closer and closer and just a little bit more...

Nanites; nanoscopic machines running around the thing like blood.

*Awareness* reaches out to me. Familiar. Comfortable. Rising from the pit of my gut, from that place where Hunt came from, where all that knowledge resides. How I knew about the thickness of the hull, the levels of nitrogen and oxygen in the atmosphere. Where the sense of danger came from. Here. It all came from here. From *that*. From the me-thing.

It does not move. Does not breathe. Doesn't have eyes or ears, but it's looking at me, reaching out to me. *Listening* to me. Not my words, but... I don't know. I can feel it, the pulse of power through its muscles, the throb of the generator in its belly.

I don't want to follow the thread, don't want to *feel* the... the thing, but there's no escaping it. It's like trying not to feel the wind against my face, the brush of hair against my cheek. The urgent, leg-crossing need to piss.

I might as well chop off my arm, or ignore the curiosity that urges me to crawl through access tubes, to curl up in the Hatchery and watch critters being made. It's impossible.

The *thing* doesn't have a name. There's a sense of identity but's it's blurry, half-formed, like it's still growing, developing. It's aware, and it *needs*, has a purpose. It's the need that's reaching out to me, hooked into my belly with that shifting multi-hued cord. A psionic umbilicus strung between us.

I wrap my fingers around it, unsure if I want to rip it out or just *feel* it. My knuckles turn white, my arm tenses. Knowledge shoots through the cord, eddies against my fist. The *awareness* cuts off. Stops.

And... nothing. Silence perhaps, a chill working its way up my spine, wrapping around my heart? A vague notion of emptiness, a hollow space in the core of me.

The *thing* fades, merging with the everything.

I let go.

Awareness and the *thing* spring back. I squeeze again.

The thing fades. Let go. Squeeze. Let go.

Fade and reappear, fade and reappear.

Awareness and curiosity, coming and going.

There's no emotion from the thing, no reproach just that *awareness* sharing knowledge with me.

I let the umbilicus go. Step back, and slip out of the eter.

Dude's still on the ceiling, nose to the ice, but he's looking at me, concentrating on *me*.

'What is it?' I ask him, only half-expecting an answer.

He keeps sniffing, swinging his muzzle back and forth, stalking whatever it is like a particularly tasty puddle of goop.

'I know you know.' I can feel it in his gaze, in the expectation. And I wonder, if I slipped into the eter and looked at Dude, really looked, what would I find.

I'm not going there though. After everything, I just need something to be easy, to be the way I expect it. The way it *should* be, the way things were before.

I clench my hands. Not that there's much chance of that, not anymore. Not with fug crawling all over my body and that... Whatever that thing was. Still connected to me, the umbilicus stretching between us, pulsing, singing. I'm trying to ignore it, but it's hard to push aside the awareness. Now that I know it's there and where it leads, it's like trying to ignore my heart, or a sun or Grea. I'd have more luck pretending I wasn't sitting in an ice tunnel, that *Citlali* wasn't being swallowed by an alien ship, and my folks weren't shit scared whenever they looked at me.

Horn's face flashes behind my eyes, the way his neck gaped open, how his parents' corpses were left to rot in their pods. At least I get some of why they were scared, and why h'Rawd looked at me like he was wondering how best to kill me.

So many questions, so few answers.

A chitter, and Dude's scurrying across the tunnel, nose still to the... I was going to say ground, but he's clinging to the walls now, and I'm wondering if those are his fug-claws or his natural ones, or maybe both, leaving tiny holes in the ice. Whichever they are, I'm starting to reconsider letting him ride on my shoulder.

Ever helpful, the HUD is outlining Dude's tracks, calculating the depth and age of them even as it tracks his progress across the ice, projecting the rest of his path down the wall and over the floor. It's kinda interesting, in a 'stop-cluttering-up-my-vision' manner, and I'm a second from ripping the mask off my face, vacuum or no, when I notice something else. There's more than one set of tracks up there.

They're outlined on the HUD too, translucent, almost invisible against the bright white of Dude's, and they're all over the place. Tiny marks in the ice, just like the critters, some shallower, some deeper, but all with the same triangular incision.

'What is it?' The words are out of my mouth, and I'm not really sure why, except the *awareness* feels a little like having Core over my shoulder. Watching. Ready to deliver the answers to the universe.

There's no response. I mean, why would there be? Whatever that thing is, it's little more than a fragment, a half-AI, if there is such a thing, and it doesn't speak my language.

I'm on my own. You'd think after everything that's happened, I'd be getting used to that.

Even if I can't make out all of what the HUD is telling me, I get the gist. And I already know, what with Dude right there, but it would be nice to hear another voice.

An army of critters marched through here.

Why? How?

Critters need oxygen just as much as the rest of us, and I'm pretty sure they don't do well in vacuum either, not without fug-armour at least.

So...

So. Given the lack of fuzzy, frozen corpses floating in the tubes, someone obviously found a way around those two problems, but why expend the resources? Hatchery would have had to grow critters especially for the job. Or bio-tanks, like the ones on Med deck.

There're Mum's words too, about critter slag sticking. What's critter slag? Some kind of vomit? And what does it do? The mystery nags at me, like a sore tooth, or a psionic umbilicus. Why? Why? Why?

*Awareness* creeps up the back of my head on soft feet, barely noticeable amongst the questions until the HUD changes. New readouts appear, big swathes of red snaking across the ice, weaving and criss-crossing like vines. Like fug vines. Like *red* fug vines.

Red fug.

As soon as the thought pops into my head, the HUD is picking up little pockets of inert nanites.

And I get it. The critters were chasing fug, but not just any fug, the *red* stuff. The same type that attacked me. I guess the critters won, or the red decided to choose another battle, because there's nothing here but ice. The HUD is tracing the inert red, and Hunt is urging me forward, my feet are following and it doesn't seem to matter where I'm going, so long as I'm following the trail.

The claw marks get thicker as I go, pock-marking the ice, changing the texture from smooth and hard, to soft and fuzzy. The nanites are getting thicker too, and soon enough little splotches of faded red coat the ceiling, the walls, and then the floor, a shadow of what was here before.

At some point, Dude lands on my shoulder, chittering his little head off. There's anger leaking from his paws, a rebuke and a sense of... wasting? I don't know, it's a new one, and right now, I've got other issues. Such as the corpse bobbing in the tunnel.

It's small. A black ball of frozen fuzz encased in plasform, like a miniature envirosuit.

The little guy's belly is shredded, the milky plasform torn, leaving room for frozen guts and globules of blood to explode out his stomach. It hovers around him in a shower of gore; the HUD picks it out in excruciating detail. Before, I would have chucked up my own guts, whatever was left in them, probably just bile by now, but the urge doesn't hit me. I feel, numb. Tired.

Dude feels more than I do. Maybe he feels for us both. Sadness joins the anger radiating from his paws, turns the bright red a dusty shade of purple.

I duck under the corpse and keep moving.

The inert red fug forms trails now, crissing and crossing just like the claw marks. I imagine vines draping from the tunnel's roof, more clinging to the sides, and giant waving reeds growing from the floor. In fact... there are cracks in the floor big enough to stick my pinky in, signs of something burrowing into the ice. They get bigger as I go along, and by the time I find the second corpse, they're big enough to stick my arm in, and the inert fug is no longer just a stain on the ice, but a thick carpet, coming up around my toes and clinging to my fug-feet.

Every step kicks a little of it into the atmosphere, until it fills the place with a fine pink fog.

I keep going, the *awareness* drawing me deeper. I have the sense we're getting close to something, whether that's *Citlali's* inner or outer hulls I'm not sure, but there's something at the end of this, something I have to see.

Dude doesn't agree with me, although the heavy brown of his disapproval has faded under the blue of mourning, every critter corpse we encounter makes it deeper, harder.

I wrap Dude in an emote, filling it with joy and warmth and my own shredded memories of being in Mum's arms. It's thin, filaments of our last encounter winding their way through what should have been happy memories, but I hope it's enough, a kind of emotional shield against the constant battery of Dude's kin turned into icicles.

The blue fades a little, replaced with pink and warmth, and there's a note of thanks, a bright yellow directed at me. It doesn't even strike me as weird anymore, that Dude knows the shield is mine, that he's even capable of sorting out what's what in the eter. If he decided to speak to me right now, in actual, human-understandable words, I wouldn't blink an eye.

For an organism bred to clean up biological junk, programmed by the kin do a single job and then die, he's pretty smart. Old Terra, if I think about it, he's pretty smart for a human too.

There's something big up ahead. The HUD is full of whatever it is, a glowing orange blob, bright at its core but not enough to burn my retinas. I can't tell whether the glow is heat or power, or both. Whatever it is, it rivals a shuttle in size. Wide and squat.

Some of that energy runs through the ice. I stop a few paces away from the first vein of it, threaded through the floor and walls in a fine web of the pale pink. It's almost not visible, a trick of the light dancing on the edges of my vision. If not for the flotilla of corpses blocking my way, I wouldn't have stopped at all.

Dude's a ball of grief. I pluck him off my shoulder and cuddle him against my chest. The fug-armour wraps around him too, like it can sense his grief, or maybe it's just reacting to my desire to shield the little fuzz butt against what comes next. I need to know what the glow is, and to do that...

At least I'm not stepping on corpses. That's one good thing about the lack of gravity, the dead critters are floating around me; for every one I push out of the way, others bump into my shoulders and legs, bobbing and twisting in my wake. They're all the same, small and black, covered in hard plasform shells, the clear bubbles cracked and shredded, spilling blood and other things into the void.

One moment I'm walking through critters, and then... The HUD is going crazy, filling the world with diagrams and readouts, and flashing yellow shapes. It's enough to make my head explode. I close my eyes, but the riot of colour is behind my lids too, Hunt whispering from my gut, parsing the shit on the HUD, and Dude—

I slam my shields in place. Everything stops, and I'm alone inside my head, just me, just the darkness behind my eyes, without even the tug of the umbilicus at my gut.

I open my eyes again. The HUD is still flashing and pulsing. I shake all the diagrams and readouts aside and rely on my own fleshy, humanoid vision. I've passed through the critters into an open space, not big, just wide enough for me to stretch my arms. It's round-ish but jagged, bits of ice sticking out at odd angles, driven into the walls and ceiling. There are massive cracks, most spreading from the ice shards, some are filled with the red fug, brighter than what I've seen before, no longer dull pink but the bright screaming red of fresh blood. The atmosphere is filled with the same colour, a frozen reddish mist.

The thing that really gets my attention are the holes in the floor and ceiling. They're huge, I could lay across them and not touch the edges. They're deep too. I can't see much, just the grooves in the sides, as if something had drilled through the ice. Something like a grappling cable.

Plasform is stuck in the roof. As if that triangular shard is a trigger, I start seeing other shards driven into the ice. I turn. Look closely at what I thought was a tunnel, at where it would have continued, at the way ice is crumbled, broken, cracked.

It dawns on me, slowly, very slowly, what some of those readouts on the HUD where telling me.

Looking at them piled on the sides of my HUD brings the readouts front and centre. They're still a confusing jumble of languages, and so I lower my shields and reach for Hunt. Understanding comes gradually, the symbols wriggling and twisting in my brain, finding places to lodge, but when it does... I want to be sick.

Vomit rockets up my throat, and it's only the thought of it hitting the faceplate and spewing back in my face that stops it erupting from my mouth.

*You figured it out,* Grea whispers in my head. *What they're using the new critters for.*

I figured it out all right, and I really wish I hadn't.

The critters escorted a bomb to this spot. It went off. They were still here.

I'm standing in vaporised critter. Blood and bone and flesh. All of it swirling around in this little crater that used to be one of Aeotu's grappling cables.

It's not that I don't get it, don't understand *why* they blew up the cable, but did they have to annihilate critters at the same time? I recall the carnage behind me, the little bodies torn apart by fug. Maybe there hadn't been a choice, maybe they had to blow the critters to free *Citlali,* but surely a drone could have done the same job.

*Why*? I'm asking Grea, but also myself. There has to be more to it.

Grea doesn't answer, is gone from my consciousness, leaving just a trace of herself behind, the cherry red clouded with secrets.

Something moves within the ice, a ribbon of orange in the black.

The ribbon pulses, once, twice, a third time. The HUD is throwing new diagrams at me, new symbols, and Hunt is translating, giving me numbers and sensor readings.

Three-point-seven metres. The thickness of the ice between me and the orange thing.

Iron, plasform and haemoglobin. The composition of the mist, of the shards embedded in the crater.

The chemical structure of the ice; hydrogen, oxygen and— That word doesn't parse, bounces off my brain. Hunt can't translate it, the word has no relation to the language I know, is something that at its core, is alien. There are other impressions, half-formed images that make no sense; a vast, grey-green tank; tiny robots splitting in half, eating and multiplying.

It's the fug. The fug is part of the ice.

There's a tug at my consciousness, a shadow of Grea, and the orange thing pulses harder, like it's acknowledging me.

Alarm, my alarm, Dude's alarm, Hunt's alarm, all of it has me backing up. My eyes are caught up in the orange pulse, stuck on it, until the HUD screams at me, and ice spews in my face, pinging off my left side as red fug erupts from the ice. I'm running then, and I'm not looking back.

Dude leads the way, and now, an hour later, I'm standing in front of another hatch. One that doesn't look like any hatch I've ever seen on Citlali, but looks a little too much like the ones on Aeotu.

I'd accuse Dude of a shit sense of direction – right after I stopped wondering how the fuck we got to Aeotu from within *Citlali's* ice hull – if there wasn't a familiar pull in my gut, a sense of Grea reaching through the hull.

There's no lock pad, no instructions, just those lines and whorls, twisting together in some kind of language, teasing the back of my brain with knowledge. And behind that... behind that, the *awareness* rises in my gut, the *thing* reaching through me, ordering the symbols, bringing understanding with it, making one of the whorls brighter than the others.

I touch it, not sure how I feel about the *thing*, now that I know what it is, or some of what it is. How I feel about the umbilicus. Still, Grea is behind the bulkhead and the lockpad is between me and whatever is on the other side. I need the... *thing*, the being on the other end of the umbilicus. For now.

The whorl wriggles under my fingers, and the *awareness* guides my hand, moving muscle and bone, twisting my wrist, spreading my index finger and thumb. The whorl moves with me, shifting, changing. Touching other lines. On my HUD, I watch heat signatures – veins of power – spread through the bulkhead, watch it find an edge, watch it describe a doorway, watch the bulkhead turn translucent, the patterns in its surface still opaque, until it resembles skin more than whatever metallic stone shit Aeotu is made of.

Even if I'd been wearing my fug-feet, the door would have been twice as tall as me, and half again as wide.

The hatch *SNAPS* back. There and then gone.

I'd seen *Them*, the aliens the kin were so afraid of, in h'Rawd's memories, knew how big they were, but still... there's nothing quite like seeing something with your own eyes to give you a better appreciation.

I don't know if these things are on a timer or have some kind of sensor, so I'm through quick smart.

The hatch *SNAPS* shut on my heels, all sign of the gaping hole gone. Just another bit of the hull.

Beyond is a room, an airlock maybe? It's small, a couple of really big strides across and a dozen more length-ways. The bulkheads are curved. *All* the bulkheads on Aeotu are curved, or at least those that I've seen, like *They* had never seen a straight line they liked. Great squishy domes, like eggs on their sides, and everywhere, the walls are carved with patterns. Shapes and lines that speak to the *thing*, that shift and change, that beckon me to follow them until the end of time.

Pain shoots through my shoulder. Small but sharp, enough to knock me out of the mesmerising effect of the pattern.

'Thanks, Dude.'

He chitters at me, reproach in his voice.

'Yeah. Yeah, I know, don't look at the walls.'

Except I have to get out of here and the patterns are the only way to do that.

That, and the *thing*.

In the short time – a full day-cycle the *awareness* tells me – I've been crawling around *Citlali*, Aeotu has changed. Power hums in the walls. I can hear it like my own heartbeat, thrumming in my ears. Warm on my flesh.

Feverish almost. I'm sweating under the fug, clammy, and there's something in the back of my throat, something that feels like that time I had the flu and Mum shoved me under the shower to bring my temperature down before rushing me off to Med.

Aeotu is sick. That knowledge pops into my brain all on its own, no help from the *awareness* required. How does a spaceship get sick?

The answer's down the next corridor.

Red and yellow-gold crawl over the bulkheads, veins of fresh-spilled blood and sunshine creeping up and over, winding in the carvings. Moving, shimmering.

The yellow-gold reminds me of the carnage in the ice hull, the shards of plasform, the traces of blown-up critters, or the tanks with their amalgamation of alien and human tech. The red though...

Fury rises off it, shimmering waves rising in the air. Not seeking, not reaching, just hanging there, hovering over the red fug like a conductor. Unlike the stuff that chased me through the ice or attacked me and Mac, there is no direction, no objective. It just sits there. Not inert or frozen but... directionless.

Dude's digging fug claws into my shoulder, and the *awareness/thing* is blaring in the back of my brain, yelling warnings, while my HUD fills with danger signs of its own. I shake them to the side, blocking the *thing* out and sending a thought to the armour on my shoulder, imagining it thicker, so thick not even Dude's fug claws can pierce it. There's something in the red fug, something that's been tickling the back of my brain. Something... strange.

Focus is my greatest talent and I use it now, stalking the red, half in and half out of the eter.

The corridor fades, not all the way, just enough so it doesn't get in the way as I focus on the red, on the way it shimmers and twists in the air.

Like when I first drew the fug into the eter, I get in close to the red, pulling it apart until the mirage is a cloud of red, thin at the edges. And like that first time, there are sparks in the depths of it, glimpses of an intelligence driving the fug. But unlike back then, when I'd been trying to stop it from destroying *Citlali*, the red doesn't attempt to trap me. It's... waiting. Unattended. Whatever is behind it, whatever drives its attack, isn't there. I sink into the cloud, burrowing deeper, chasing the sparks of lightning buried in its core.

They're faint, distant, thick with the sense of waiting.

I reach out to bring the sparks closer and... There. A pause, a moment of nothing and then... and then... The lightning is gone. Disappeared, leaving the faint scent of ozone and... cherries? I grab for it again, the lingering aftertaste of the intelligence behind the red. It stains the eter, trips a memory of home, of Mum and Grea, smoke pouring out of the cooker and—

It's gone. Vanished from the eter like it never was.

There's a shiver in my spine, caught there.

I pull out of the eter, and know, deep in the pit of me, that this isn't going to end well.

# CHAPTER THIRTEEN

The sickness gets worse the deeper into Aeotu I go. Every couple of steps I forget I'm on Aeotu, that the corridors aren't Citlali's, that I'm not in some weird dream or kin-built psionic hallucination. Fug covers the bulkheads, crawls over the curving ceiling and trails across the deck but instead of the grey-green, it's a bright screaming red. The yellow's in there too, thin filaments of the stuff winding around the red, but it's the red that makes my skin crawl.

Menace rolls off it, beating like a heart.

Maybe it's the way it feels like Grea but not. Maybe, too, it's the way that Grea's presence gets stronger as the red grows thicker, as the rage lifting off it chokes the air. Maybe it's Dude vibrating on my shoulder, or the *awareness* growing behind my eyes. Maybe it's the sense of Aeotu behind the *awareness*. Maybe.

Whatever it is, I keep moving forward.

I'm standing before a familiar hatch, the membrane snapping back into the deck. Behind is another familiar corridor, thinner with just two doors; one at the end, the other just a few paces in. The end one leads to Aeotu's core, to the only colour, besides the red fug, that I've ever seen on the ship. The other door...

Grea's behind it.

My hand lifts of its own accord, hovering over the hatch.

I can feel her. It's different than before, than when I stood in front of *Citlali's* engines and felt the cherry-red of her presence. That was a breeze, a gentle brush of silk against my skin. This is a gale pressing not just into my palm but into *all* of me, demanding my attention. My presence.

The hatch snaps downwards.

Beyond is darkness.

In the corner of my eye, Dude disappears.

{{ *Danger,* }} the *awareness* whispers.

I step over the threshold.

Not even the HUD can penetrate the black, but there's a map in front of me, a three-dimensional layout of the room – the command centre, *awareness* says – a ghost guiding me around waist-high workbenches and triangular pads atop tall poles that might be stools.

There's a *SSSNAP* from behind as the hatch closes, and then light. I'm blind, holding my hands up against the glare. Tears blur my vision, but a couple of blinks and I can make out the central holo blazing like a sun, casting the double ring of workbenches into stark shadow.

'Grea?' I say, and am surprised my voice doesn't echo.

'Hey, fathead.' She steps out of the shadows beyond the holo.

I can't help it. I step back. Horror has claws in my chest, flaming talons sunk deep into my heart. I try hold it back, but there's that second, that split-moment before I take control, before reason raises its voice and tells me that's my twin. My sister. The other half of my soul.

A split-moment is all it takes. There are no secrets between Grea and me. I don't know what it's like with others, twins or siblings or empaths, any of those. I just know, that in the moment before I slammed my shields in place and reeled back the emotion roiling in my core, that Grea felt it. Know that it hurt, worse than if I'd launched myself across the decking and ripped her face off.

Nothing shows in her expression. It never does. Grea's got control like I've got focus, got denial down to a fine art. Her face looks exactly as she wants it, when she wants it, and right now... Right now there's a pleasant smile curving her lips, making her eyes twinkle, but the rest of her... Pain rolls between us, a great well of it filling the space.

'That's not nice, Kuma.'

'I'm sorry.'

'You should be.' She steps farther out of the shadows, skin sliding out of the blackness, catching the light from the holo and throwing it back. 'I'm not that hideous. Not like you.'

That last one is a laser-guided missile aimed at my heart. It hits, like she intended. And I let it, feel it spread under my skin. It's only fair.

And she's right, she's not hideous, she's just... Different doesn't cover it. I want to say that fug has done to her what it's done to me, but that wouldn't be true, wouldn't cover the extent of the changes. The girl standing in front of me... she's not the girl from the eter, not the twin I remember. She's older, maybe older than me, and the fug... The fug hasn't given her paws or slicked her skin in the shiny black of Mac's armour. Hasn't changed her fingers to spikes, it's... It's hard to describe. She's Grea, but she's not. Her face has changed. Her nose is wider, flatter, and there's a glow about her shoulders, an aura like she's generating light from inside herself. A holo made flesh.

I can deal with all that, can be jealous over the way her skin shimmers and her eyes glow, it's the wave of red falling from her shoulders that turns my stomach. It writhes and twists, a million thin tendrils of fug bound together; bits of it separate from the whole to curl around her neck, caress her cheek, twine through her hair. Grea turns, and for a second I can see a bald spot at the base of her skull and the red buried there.

I stumble back.

'What happened to you?'

Grea smiles. She's in front of me and I'm not quite sure how that happened. One moment she was on the other side of Command and now she's holding out her hand.

Out of Mac and I, Grea is the one who looks most like my

memories of her. The fug hasn't made her taller or given her paws, and if I don't look at the cape, don't follow it into the darkness, I can almost pretend that nothing has changed, except... Except she doesn't *feel* like my twin anymore.

Dude is fuzzing, the warm gold of his presence threaded with the sharp bite of danger, a bite the *other* in the pit of me echoes.

Nonetheless, this is Grea. My other half, and she's waiting for me.

I take her hand.

And wish I hadn't.

That feeling, that sense that Grea isn't Grea anymore, is bolting up my arm, twisting under my skin.

Yanking my hand back is instinctive, like snatching your hand from a flame, except Grea holds on.

Fear, cold as the void, grips my heart. 'Let go.'

'You're scared of me?' It's a statement breathed on a question, riding the air between us on a wave of disbelief, hurt and—

I'm not touching that last emotion. Not. Touching. It.

The *awareness* is blaring in my ear. Danger. Danger. Danger!

There's something in my throat, tying up my vocal cords, making it hard to breathe. I think it's my heart. And still... and still... This is Grea.

I tug on my hand. 'Let go of me, Grea. Please.'

Her fingers tighten on mine, and that red fug is oozing over her flesh, wrapping around my fingers, extending over my knuckles, creeping up my wrist. Digging in.

The pain is sharp, hot, and behind it, seeping in through the blood trickling from the slices in my skin, is that thing, that thing I'm not going to touch because if I do, Grea won't be Grea anymore and I won't be able to pretend.

She pulls me close so our noses are touching. 'Why?' she says.

'Why what?'

'Why pretend? Am I so terrible as I am?'

I jerk back, as far as my captive hand will go. 'You read me.'

She cocks her head. 'You're my brother. The other half of me.'

'What happened to you?'

'You did. Or you happened to Aeotu and then Aeotu happened to us and then Euiva happened to me.'

Everything stops. Me. The *awareness*. Aeotu.

Euiva. The name echoes, brings memories of a pulsing metal shield hidden in a bulkhead, of sharing Aeotu's mind as she recalled the last time she saw the sister ship. The flat-nosed aliens the kin called *Them* scurrying through emergency docking tubes, evacuating Euiva as her internal systems turned against them, her airlocks leaking atmosphere, her engines failing. *Their* hands on Aeotu's controls, releasing the tubes, forcing her away, leaving her crippled sister-ship to die alone in the void.

*Sister*, Aeotu whispers and for once she's not referring to me.

I shiver. 'Euvia? As in the beacon in Dad's lab?'

'Who else would I mean?'

I shake my head. 'But… it's just a beacon. From a dead ship.'

'No, not dead just not…' Grea shrugs. 'Not close enough. When you found the beacon, Euiva was too far away to communicate but then Aeotu began moving, and as we got closer I felt it. I saved it. '

A pause and then, 'Why?'

'Because she's in pain. Can't you feel it?' She presses her other hand to my chest. 'Don't you want to help?'

The red rushes over her hand, long wicked tendrils aimed at my heart. I wrench myself out of her grip. She lets me go and I stumble backward, eyes glued to the red barbs twisting around her wrist.

Grea cocks her head to the side. I've never felt like a bug under a microscope before. 'It's okay, baby brother, I understand. Aeotu got her hooks in you first, or was it you who got your hooks into Aeotu?' She shakes her head. 'It doesn't matter, it's all the same in the end.'

There's a war going on in my brain, between the half of me desperate to find my sister, and the half that's telling me the person standing before me isn't her. If I run, twist around in the dark and sprint, can I get the hatch open before the thing behind Grea's eyes gets me?

Dude is silent, invisible, and the *awareness* whispers: no.

It wouldn't matter if it whispered yes, I tell it and the half of myself that is scared shitless of the red, of Euiva. I have to save Grea.

I stop shuffling back, stand straight. 'So, you're saving a spaceship. How? When?'

'You woke me up, and then I heard Aeotu. After Stasis separation, when Core ejected you into space; the fug held the deck together, and I managed to get out and find you.' Her face darkens. 'I knew what I had to do when I saw what it was doing to you and Mac, what it had done to everyone else. I was going to try and restart Core, get the drones back online but…'

Remembered pain stains the air around Grea. 'Core was gone, and Ag… Ag was crazy. The Lab AI was okay for a while, and Med. We did what we could, but with Core gone everything just fell apart, and then Aeotu jumped to FTL and I *still* couldn't get Mum or Dad out of their pods and—'

She breaks off, and I watch her chest rise as she takes a deep breath, watch her control herself. 'But it was okay.' Grea smiles, the expression is big and bright but I can see the lie, the pain dogging her heels. 'Because that was when I heard Euiva, and together we did this.' She gestures down at herself, and then the red.

'I don't…' Don't see it. Don't like it. Would have freaked the fuck out already if it weren't for Dude on my shoulder and the stubborn insistence that this was Grea.

'That's okay, baby brother. I get it. I do. Besides, it's a bit dark in here. Let me put all the lights on.' Red, a bright candy-coloured blood lights up the darkness. Thick veins of it, pulsing on the walls, trailing over the deck, twining around Grea's ankle...

'Red fug.' There's so much of it, enough to swim in, and all of it leading back to my sister.

'Viyusa actually.' Grea picks it up, and the tendril curls around her hand. Lovingly. Gently. Like a puppy trying to get closer to her skin. 'There wasn't enough left in Euiva's beacon, not to do what we needed, so we adapted Aeotu's viyu.'

My confusion must show on my face, because Grea tilts her head and gives me that smile, the one I hate, the one that says I'm a little slow but that's okay, because she's there to fix shit for me.

'The stuff you call fug?' She points at me, taking in my fug-feet and hands. 'The nanites that form your armour? It's called viyu. Aeotu grows it the same way our bodies make blood cells. It's part of what she is.'

'It's a spaceship.'

A hand on her hip, a shift of the light, and suddenly the old Grea, *my* Grea is standing before me. If I just ignore the tendrils. 'Really? Four years in the grow field and you haven't figured it out yet?' She bops my forehead, palm pushing my head back on my neck.

I push away, feel the scowl creasing my brow and the same old anger that always came after she did that rises in the air between. 'Don't—' That's when it hits me. The number. 'Four years? What do you mean, "four years"?'

'What it sounds like, Kuma.' She says it slowly, holding her hand up, lifting one finger and then another. 'One. Two. Three. Four revolutions around Jørn's solar body. I mean, I think so. The chronometers have been a little screwy ever since we hit FTL.'

'FTL.' Grea mentioned it before, but it hadn't really sunk in and now... Now I nod, because really, nodding's the only motion I'm capable of while my brain scrambles to catch up.

'Yeah. Aeotu powered the engines about a year after the merge.' Grea's not looking at me anymore, she's turned to the command console, her hands working at the boards. 'I tried to stop it, but I couldn't fix Core's connections with the sub-AIs and there's only so much you can do with a Franken-thrower. Seriously, fathead, cool invention but next time maybe make it a little less bulky, 'cause it sucks carrying three of those things around.'

'Try crawling through an air duct.'

'Oh, I did that. It's almost as bad as dragging them through the cyclers, that recycled goop gets everywhere.'

Grea's still not looking at me, fiddling with the control board, hands passing through the symbols projected above it, moving smoothly, as if she knows what she's doing.

For a long, tense minute neither of us speak.

Grea's the one to break the silence. 'I tried to find you after Aeotu brought you in, but there was so much viyu in the way and half of *Citlali* was vacuum, and then, when I got there, and saw what she was doing...' The blood drains from Grea's face, all the warmth leaving her skin, leaving it grey under the gold. One moment I'm looking at my sister, the next... The thing that made me step back from her in horror is looking out at me. It has Grea's eyes, her hair, her mouth... It reminds me of Aeotu under my twin's face but the look is cold. It's rage. It's calculation. All the things Grea has never been. Until now.

I can't help it, I slip into the eter, just a little. I have to know. Peeking under Grea's skin is the only way.

The psionic plane seethes with darkness. Not the black of lies but true darkness, like a piece of the ora is bleeding through reality, staining the endless white, but then... it's not that either. There's no sense of possibility, of creation. It's just... blank. Nothing. I don't want to touch it.

The darkness spreads behind Grea, a shifting cloak blowing on an invisible breeze. Grief, the remembered kind, muted by time, twists around her feet, and something else. Red strands that remind me of the gold veins under my own skin, the ones that connect to Dude, they snake around Grea, not quite touching but hovering. I follow it, away from Grea and into the darkness, a line of blood trailing into the shadows, connecting to another presence.

Following it further means touching the shadows. And Grea is looking at me, not the fleshy me, but the psionic me. Her head tilted in a not-quite human fashion that makes my skin crawl.

She frowns. 'I told you that wasn't nice, baby brother.'

'Sorry,' I say. Although I'm not, not really. It's just... I'm staring down a predator and there's this feeling that if I make the wrong move, she's going to pounce.

'Euiva got the idea from you.' Grea glides closer. 'From what Aeotu was doing to you. I burned my way into the grow field.' The space between us fills with the smooth walls of not-*Citlali*, the off-white flowing into the dark grey of what I guess is the place I woke up. I guess that, because in the middle of it all, on the other side of memory-Grea – feet braced, a dozen drones hovering around her, shooting lasers into the fug even as the Franken-thrower spews a solid beam of hard light – is a memory of me. As Grea lowers the Franken, the memory zooms in, focusing on my face, on the mounds of fug layered over me, on the golden flesh of my feet, toes swallowed by the beginnings of a talon.

'I tried to get you out.' Desperation colours the memory, casting it in shades of violent green, as memory-Grea rushes forward, a multi-tool appearing in her hand. 'But I was in Aeotu's heart, the place where she's strongest. Where the viyu is strongest. I burned and I burned and I burned, but it just kept coming back.' Between us, Grea cries and shouts, as she points the multi-tool at the fug holding me down, the hot line of the laser eating at the nanites. And the nanites grow back as fast as she burns. The desolation in her voice stabs me in the heart. Over and over.

Around us, the drones dodge and weave, holding back the wave of fug launching itself at her back. One explodes and then another and another, until there's just two left.

'The drones couldn't hold it off.' Grea, the real Grea, walks toward me, the memory moving around her. 'We had to go.'

Memory-Grea runs.

'I was angry with Aeotu, after. Why was she doing this to you? She had stopped talking to me, and so I had to find out on my own. It took me awhile, a few months maybe, until I found the beacon.' The memory changes. Grea is on Lab Two burning fug with the Franken, another drone bobbing behind her. Grea looks different, her hair longer, her face thinner, and her eyes... There's a coldness in them.

One moment she'd been burning fug, the next a familiar bulkhead is sliding aside, revealing a shield, pulsing like it's alive.

Memory-Grea touches it and red fu— viyusa spills around her hand.

'I heard her,' the real Grea says. 'Heard Euiva as I had heard Aeotu. The distance between her and the beacon made her weak and the only way she could help me was with the viyusa.'

Red swallows memory-Grea, crawling up her arm, over her shoulder, plunging into her skull—

The memory ends, leaving the real Grea a hairsbreadth from my nose. 'I knew what I had to do after that; fight nanites with nanites.'

Grea spreads her arms. Light gleams on her nanite skin, all the colours in the universe rippling under the surface. 'Med helped, before she went offline. They're just nanites after all, but it wasn't until Euiva became stronger that I really figured things out.

'There's more to this than just me, than us,' Grea continues. She's sharing my breath, her aura mixing with mine. 'She needs us, Kuma. *They* need us. Arthur Tudor knew it, felt it when he found the beacon and then the kin killed him when he tried to do something about it.'

'What do you know about AD Tudor?'

'Everything.' She leans in close, not just physically but psionically, slipping into my memories, finding the confrontation with Onah, the memories I'd stolen. 'He wasn't just an empath, Kuma, he was a *Regan*-level empath. We might not be able to cross lightyears to touch another mind, but he could and he did. He slipped out of stasis/sleep and tapped into *Citlali's* generators not to blow us up, but to use Euiva's beacon and reach across the stars.

'It's working, Kuma. I'm pushing back Aeotu. I even got into her systems. I haven't been able to alter anything yet, just watch, but we're working on it, and soon...' She turns away, suddenly, her eyes focused behind, on something in the darkness, and her lips... they move. No words come out, but she's speaking. Speaking to the darkness.

'What's in there?'

'Just Euiva.'

'The beacon?'

'No.' She draws the word out, like she does when she thinks I'm being particularly thick. 'Euiva. I told you.'

'Euiva's a ship, Grea, and even if it's *not* dead, we're not Tudor, we can't reach across lightyears; trying to reach her psionically would kill you.' I point at the darkness, at the thing I can almost sense within it. 'Whatever you're talking to, it can't be Euiva.'

Her eyes narrow, turn to slits. I know that look, or a version of it, a version without the malice dripping like acid from her pores. 'Are you calling me crazy?'

'You're talking to a dead thing.'

She stalks forward. 'Why are you doing this?'

'Something's wrong with you.'

'Something's wrong with you too, baby brother. Or haven't you looked down lately?'

Her hand's on my arm, those too-long fingers wrapping around my bicep, pulling me close physically and psionically. Wrapping under my skin. I can't move. One second, I'm my own person, the next that sick thing within Grea is winding through my blood, seeking out the golden threads that connect me to Dude and—

Rage hits me. A fine web of gold sweeping over my shoulder, drawing power from the *other* in my gut. A tidal wave crashing through my blood, my bones, sweeping over the darkness with fire.

A scream. High. Piercing. Like burning fug. It dives into my ears, a dagger carving up my grey matter, slicing through thought and reason until the only thing I feel, think, know, is that I can't let the thing within Grea touch me.

I rip myself away. Stumble back, fug-feet tripping over themselves, shock and that lingering darkness making them clumsy. The viyusa is still burning through my skin, making the armour loose. Numb.

Grea's on the deck, still screaming, the sound piercing my eardrums, clawing at my chest. Red pulses under her skin; violent, crazy flashes of lightning cracking down her arms, over her back, and behind her... The red fug— The viyusa roils, tendrils and veins writhing in the shadows, slapping the deck, screaming on their own. But it's the thing on the eter, the stain, that stops my heart and has the first icy skewer of real fear, the kind that creeps up on you, that your mind tries to push back, to cover up with denial. The kind of fear that comes before everything, *everything* changes, and not for the better.

The thing is looking at me. There are no eyes, no face, nothing but an intense focus, an attention reaching through the rip between realities. There's familiarity in it, in the tiny glimpse of vastness, the multi-hued alienness that reminds me of Aeotu. But it's not Aeotu, doesn't have the same welcome. No, this thing is cold as the void, driven and merciless in the way few things truly are.

Euiva.

*Sister.* Aeotu is standing in front of me. Not just the sense of her, or her voice, but *her*, a solid humanoid form in the eter, shielding me from Euiva. She looks like Mac in his fug-armour, the same sleek body and featureless head, hands ending in talons, but where he is solid black, Aeotu ripples with colour.

No other words pass between us, but knowledge, images, memories wash over me, things she's never shown me before, things that shake me all the way to my anima. They find places in my brain, and now... Now I understand. Now I know, and that fear, that sense of changing, of doom, solidifies in my gut.

I take one last look at Grea, and run.

# CHAPTER FOURTEEN

Running away from my sister doesn't make me feel good. Doesn't make me feel like a hero or a brother or a decent, everyday person. Running away when she's in pain, screaming her guts out on the deck, makes me feel worse. A coward, a heel, a right fucking bastard. The self-loathing is rich, winds its way up through my stomach and curdles the acid, makes me want to vomit.

It doesn't stop me sprinting the other way though, back through Aeotu's ovoid hallways to the crumbled husk of *Citlali*. Doesn't stop me from scrambling down access tubes, using the ladders where I can, using my fug-claws where the rungs built into the tubes are eaten away to nothing. I use the claws more often than not. I've gotten good at it.

The first time the side of a tube crumbled under my hand, sending me sliding all the way down, only reflex saved me. That, and a little help from Dude. I'd shot arms and legs out, trying to find purchase on the smooth sides, grabbing at lower rungs, at air, at anything that might slow my meeting with the deck twenty metres below. Dude had done the rest, his smooth, calm gold shooting through the web under my skin. I'd half-sensed the command he used, the image of a critter climbing a bulkhead, and then my fingers were plunging in the steelcrete, shredding the metal like skin, and slowing my headlong rush into broken bones.

Coordinating feet and hands had taken awhile, retracting claws and griping with them. Now, the muscles in my arms and back screamed, while the ones in my thighs, where the armour was thickest, felt like they could go on forever. If I was lucky, forever wouldn't be required.

A light on the top of my head picks out the junction ahead, just a few more handholds and I'll be on Lab Two, or what's left of it. From what I've seen of the rest of the ship, Aeotu hasn't been kind to *Citlali*. The signs of fug are everywhere, and I wonder what the alien ship has in store for the thing it thinks is home. Or does it?

Before Core shot me into space in an escape pod, the AI said Aeotu was repairing *Citlali*. So what changed?

The thing in my gut, the knowledge that passed between Aeotu and I in the eter, tells me it was Grea, the part of her that touched Euiva. If Grea hadn't woken up, hadn't tried to save me from the grow field, then this wouldn't be happening.

I'm climbing into the junction, my arms strings of old biogel, legs powering me along. There's no time to stop. I have to save Grea, and there's only one way I know, that *Aeotu* knows to do that.

On my shoulder, Dude is silent. Almost too silent, none of his usual golden fuzz singing in the back of my brain, and I'm wondering what that is, what it means as a way of not thinking about what's coming up. What I'm going to find.

I punch out of the maintenance tube, literally. Fug-feet tearing through the steelcrete, the fug-eaten metal giving way with a metallic sigh.

Lab Two looks just as I remember. Plain, off-white corridors curving ever so slightly, doors inset in the bulkheads. It's colder than when I was here last, cold enough I feel it through my shipsuit, ice crawling under my skin, freezing my bones. Fug-armour flows over my hands and arms, covers the parts of me it had left bare, and slowly, warmth chases off the cold. Numbers are flashing on the HUD, blinking on the side of my vision. Temperature and atmosphere readings telling me that I really don't want to be here without the armour, or an EVA suit. At least gravity is still working. A small mercy when I'm not at risk of plunging to my death in a maintenance tube.

There's a map on my HUD too, white lines outlining the corridor ahead, a yellow one guiding me to the right, around the curve of the corridor. I shouldn't need it. I know this deck like the back of my hand. Or I used to. Four years and fug have done things to my old stomping ground, demolished bulkheads and made craters in the decking, formed new walls and arches, turned the place into a maze.

Most of the fug here is the dull, grey-green of inert nanites, still clinging to the bulkheads and ceiling. Some of it litters the deck, a grey dust that puffs under my feet, mixing with crumbled steelcrete and plasform. It's everywhere and getting thicker as I follow the guide, winding my way through the reconstructed deck, climbing through gaps in the bulkheads and over the remnants of work benches and hover stools. There's less of the dead stuff here, more of the grey-green; thick ropes of it strung across the corridor, a thicker carpet advancing along the walls, the floor.

A low, inaudible growl rumbles through my skin.

I stop, alarm rising. 'Dude?'

He's standing at attention, a rigid statue of a mini rucnart on my shoulder, his barbed tail curled over his back and pointed at something ahead of us; a little, fug-grown missile.

The HUD is clear, just the outlines of the bulkheads and the yellow line guiding me past the curtain of fug ahead. A curtain of fug. Yeah. Okay. I remember the last curtain I pushed through. The alarm ratchets up another notch. I take a breath, feel the blades slide over my knuckles, and advance.

The curtain parts like it's been waiting for me. I slip through. Adrenalin has my heart beating hard and my lungs sucking down air. There's a readout on my HUD, tracking the uptick in my pulse and the oxygen saturation of my blood. There's a readout for the shit on the other side of the curtain too, and a little display just under it showing me the curtain falling shut on my heels.

Because of the other red shit. The viyusa.

The corridor with its off-white walls doesn't look like a corridor anymore.

I'm standing in a battlefield of fug. Red and grey-green clashing in slow-motion, shifting back and forth, eating bulkheads and ceilings and the deck. It's a duo-toned dance of death, red and green killing each other, dissolving into piles of dust.

There's not a skerrick of off-white to be seen, not a straight line or an arch that looks like a door. It's an endless field of destruction. An alien landscape where the only familiar things are the outlines on my HUD showing me what was, and that yellow line guiding me forward.

I plunge into the chaos.

My fug-armour is shifting, thickening over my knees, forming hard plates up my spine, turning feet and hands into weapons.

I'm not sure it needed to bother. The viyusa is slow, moving like it's stuck in a time dilation field, just a few nano-seconds after me but it's fast enough. A coil of it falls in front of me, a vine the length of my whole body, and thick as my leg. Behind it, another and another. A forest of red, wavy stalactites with pointy ends looking for a fug-fleshy Kuma to wrap up and tear apart. Distantly, I'm aware of the armour thickening still more, new plates forming over my shoulders and chest, slinking down my arms, of bony ridges growing on my knuckles, while Dude hunkers down.

Hunt rises on the adrenalin, calm taking over the hot bubble of panic, clearing my mind and narrowing my focus until all I see are those vines. The fug blades slice through the first, I'm already past it, noting in the same way I noted the armour shifting, that it's still moving, my blade not going all the way through. I'm swinging at the next, ducking under another as it tries to wrap around my arm, a nano-second too slow. Slice, run, duck, slice. Again and again.

The vines are getting thicker, and the yellow line... My destination isn't any closer. I'm swinging and cutting, Hunt moving my arms, twisting and turning my body. Dude's growling, and I can feel him too, bending my knees when a new vine slashes at it, making me jump and twist. There's red in the readouts on my HUD, warnings, swirls and lines, and then I feel it, the burning. Pain blazes up my forearms from the fug blades, a long line of red eating into my flesh, seeking my bones. Inside the shell of Hunt, I scream; scream until I have no breath left, and then I scream some more, but Hunt... Hunt doesn't stop moving, Dude doesn't stop picking up my feet or slashing with the blades.

Viyusa coats the cutting edge of the blades, a thin pink skin creeping over the green, eating it. It's oozing over my knuckles, pooling in hollows between tendons and branching out, thin filaments of it creeping over the armour, each one burning, eating. And still Hunt keeps me moving, keeps me following that yellow line.

The forest of red is getting thicker, more vines dropping from the ceiling, every single one intent on me. I'm not going to make it, not going get to Dad's old lab, not going to reach the beacon hidden in the secret compartment at the back. The one AD Tudor died to protect. The one that led to this whole broken mess.

The last piece of a dying ship.

The thing I need to kill.

Except I'm not moving forward anymore. The HUD is screaming warnings, Hunt is turning me around, and Dude... Dude is doing whatever it is the critter thinks he needs to do. Keeping me alive. Maybe. But I can't stop now, I have to get to Dad's lab. If I'm going to save Grea, it's time for me to take control.

Taking control is easier said than done. Hunt has me bundled up in the back of my own skull, a passenger, and Dude... He's taking part like a master puppeteer, I can feel him underneath my skin, ringing through the golden web, and if I concentrate hard enough, I can even feel *him*. Not his presence, but his physical self, claws out, body vibrating with tension, I can even feel his second pair of front legs, like they're attached to my ribs. It's weird, but it's a start.

A start is all I need.

While Hunt twists and turns and slashes, retreating back the way we've come, I slip into the eter and reach for Dude. He's a little gold blob in the white, sitting in the centre of his web. Attention streaks out from his paws in blazing white lines, each one connected to a ghost of fug-me, dancing in the eter. It's jarring to see me fighting for my life and to not feel it. Most of it is not being in control, of knowing that I'm an optional extra in the function of my own body, but the other part... The other part is still not recognising myself, the height, the breadth of shoulder, the alienness of the fug armour. I might have stared at myself in the eter, might have had a chance to know, intellectually, that that's me, but I don't feel it, not right in the pit of myself where identity lives.

'Dude?'

The blazing lines of attention shiver.

'Dude?' I say again, this time reaching out to touch him in the middle of his web. 'I have to keep going.'

One of those lines shifts, reaches for me. Touching it is like sticking my hand in an open subline, a rush of power straight to the heart. Holy Terra, the little guy packs a punch, or maybe not... There's that thing behind him, the heart that isn't mine. Hunt. I can see it now, a ghost behind Dude, the growl of its generator echoes through the critter, fills the eter, reaches through the web at Dude's paws and powers my limbs.

I sink my fingers into the web and claim Hunt's power for myself. Control is mine.

I jerk back to the world, still feeling Dude under my skin, Hunt watching in the back of my eyes, but I'm here. No longer a passenger.

Viyusa is everywhere, the pain of it digging at my bones, turning my marrow to mush. It blinds me, and this time my scream rings through the corridor, a blood-curdling screech. Only Dude and Hunt keep me going while my nerves burn, push the agony back, give me room to breathe, to think, to act.

I spin, no longer retreating, but forging ahead. I run, leaping over severed stalactites still writhing on the deck, and there is the remembered gouge from where I rammed a hover sled into the wall that feels like a lifetime ago, before fug. Next to it, half-obscured by the viyusa, is the door to Dad's lab. Hope blooms in my chest.

Not far, not far. The HUD measures the distance, the numbers switching between English numerals and the lines of Hunt, fritzing around the edges like it can't quite decide which language to use. It doesn't matter, with Hunt sharing my eyes, I can read them both. Ten metres.

I'm going to make it, I going to make—

The deck crumbles, steelcrete giving way like a sinkhole, opening beneath me mid-leap.

Red slashes across my vision. The HUD screams in my ear. Viyusa vines whip toward me, and the big dark hole rushes at my feet.

Oh shit.

I plunge into darkness.

✳

The darkness burns. Acid in my lungs, creeping through my muscles, eating my nerves.

I scream until my throat is raw, and then I scream some more.

There are bands around my arms, my legs, my ribs. They squeeze and contract, the ones around my chest do it every time I yell, like they're helping to squeeze every last bit of air from lungs.

Eventually, the pain subsides. Or maybe I get used to it because I stop screaming. At some point in the interminable hours, days, weeks, I've been in the darkness, I found that place Hunt shoved me when it took over my body. The pain was still there, still eating me, but it wasn't me it was happening to, wasn't me who screamed until his voice broke.

Dude is huddled in here with me, in the away place. I'm pretty sure he screamed too, his little voice high and piercing, drowned beneath my own. The only one who doesn't scream is Hunt. It sits in the back of my mind, behind my eyeballs, watching, calculating.

*That wasn't nice, little brother.* Grea, reaching out through the viyusa. *Trying to kill Euiva.*

*I was saving you.*

*What makes you think I need saving?* She's hovering in the darkness, a part of it. And where before the darkness was a cloak at her feet, now it's the red, tendrils of it draped over her shoulders and head like a cowl.

*Euiva is controlling you, changing you.*

*And you think Aeotu isn't doing the same to you? Hasn't* already *done it?*

*She hasn't.*

*What about Hunt?* She pulls the memory from the back of my brain, of the *awareness* moving me through fug.

*That's different.*

*How?* Grea's face is in mine, our foreheads touching.

*It was helping me.*

*And Euiva's not helping me?* Grea cocks her head. *She helped me save you, brother.*

*She's destroying our home!*

*Our home is already dead.* Grea's in my face and the darkness is twisting around my legs, trying to find its way under my skin. *We're giving it another life, another purpose.*

*What?*

*Did I stutter?* Grea moves toward me, not walking but gliding, pulling the red with her, around her, a swirling mass of... Of something I really don't want to touch me. *All this, it's not about you or me or even Aeotu and Citlali anymore, it's about the Sisters.*

Sisters. The word echoes, and for a brief moment I hear Aeotu.

*Who are the Sisters?*

Grea smiles and the expression... chills. She smacks me on the forehead and knowledge shoots through her palm, drowning me in images and emotions. Part memory, part something else... something that comes from the red. It wraps around me like the vines, but instead of clamping around my arms or my chest, it sinks into the heart of me, seeking out my anima. It hurts, hurts just the same as the viyusa, burning, eating. Acid poured on all of the tender places.

Dude's growling, chasing it, hunting it down. It gets him too.
*Stop!*

*I'm showing you, brother.*

*You're hurting us. You're* letting *it hurt us.*

Grea is everywhere, riding in on the thread that connects us as twins, that makes us the same. *It's the only way,* she says.

There's another memory overlaying the pain, one of Grea, curled in a ball, alone, only the light of a drone for company. Her face it grey, and her lips are bleeding, but it's the whimpers that dig at my soul, that make my heart clench. I want to tell her I don't want it, whatever this knowledge is. I don't need it, she can just *tell* me, but there's that look on her face. The cold, hard thing, and behind it... behind it there's Euiva, and all that pain, all that loneliness is hers.

It eats at me. I'm trying to hold it off, fighting it with hands that shake. Blood running down my fingers. And Dude... the worst is Dude – the sound he's making, the high, quiet whine drilling into my heart, splitting it in two. One half for me, the other for my twin.

My twin. Who's looking at me with Euiva behind her eyes, without mercy, without anything that I remember as her.

*No.* The word is less a word than a force, a denial pushing outward from my anima. A shield. *No,* I say again, and this time it ripples through the stuff that makes me *me.* I gather it to me, make it stronger, harder. I yell it. *No!*

The emote takes flesh and bone with it as it rips Euiva from my psyche.

Grea screams. Rage fills the air, frustration. Fear. Loneliness.

She stumbles back through the dark, the viyusa clinging to her, the emotion/memory flung in her face, bright, hot. Burning.

She disappears.

# CHAPTER FIFTEEEN

Aeotu sweeps me up.

I'm tumbling through the kaleidoscope of her mind. It's different from the last time I was here, more… natural, I guess. Easier. Before I was a Kuma-coloured bubble in Aeotu's mind, struggling to keep myself on the river that rages toward her core, pulled this way and that by the tributaries that branch off the main thrust of her thoughts. This time the river doesn't threaten to drown me, doesn't batter my shields.

The tributaries, the fragments of Aeotu's self, still call to me, want to tell me things like hull pressure and oxygen ratios, but they don't tug, don't fight over my attention. It's Aeotu herself, the core of her, who guides my path, nudging me away from the river that leads directly to her anima, toward a smaller tributary singing with the warm bronze of home.

I don't know what I'm expecting, what a ship calls home. A drydock? A massive steelcrete skeleton orbiting a moon? Whatever it is, it's not the glittering bronze web, a constellation of minds thrumming to the same beat as Aeotu's, an interconnectedness like what I have with Grea, except closer. It's the Sisters, the other ships like Euiva. And they're all gone, the stars dark, only the memory of them left behind, the places where they used to be, faint glows kept alive in Aeotu's memory. All except one.

One of the stars is alight, a crimson glow. Not as it was, but alive. Joy fills the space, pain too. Aeotu's emotions swirl around me, not crushing but buffeting me in their wake.

The tide of Aeotu's mind pushes me closer and closer to that glow, and I'm pretty sure I don't want to reach it, 'cause I know what's there, know deep in the pit of me.

Euiva.

The dark net in my way is a relief.

The web is strung across the rushing tide of Aeotu's sub-mind in strands of black fug. Menace rolls off it, like the darkness that surrounded Grea. It pulses with old memories and fear, has its own gravity, a pull that has me reaching for it, even as the sane part of me, the bit that used to wake in the middle of the night convinced of the bogeyman in the wall units, recoils.

I grab a strand. It's midnight in my grip, the absolute cold of the void, the despair of floating in the stasis unit, waiting to die. The strand twists around my wrist, slowly at first, hesitant, like it doesn't know what to make of me. For a moment, it *tastes* me, rolls my essence around its mouth. I think it likes what it finds because the strand tightens on my arm, lifts me from the tributary. My feet are dangling above the flow of Aeotu's consciousness until the tips of my toes brush the surface.

There are new waves, black crests in the darkness. Fear is universal, it seems, and it stains Aeotu's thoughts. It's an old fear, rising from the depths of her being with threads tracing all the way back to her core.

But here... Here doesn't feel like a part of Aeotu. It's different, the blackness a foreign body embedded not just in the AI's psyche, but trailing through the constellation behind it. Sticky little tendrils reaching out to each of the withered, faded stars of the Sisters.

The vines wrap tighter around my arm, and now more of them are coming out of the dark, twining around my waist, my legs, my shoulders, encasing me. That little part of my brain, scared of the bogeyman, is whimpering, curled up on itself, hands over its head, calling for Dad, but it's far away, hidden behind layers of... home? Not Aeotu's home – the constellation of minds – but *my* home, or what's meant to be my home. The planet where my parents were born, Jørn.

Giant trees reaching for blue skies; the endless push and pull of ocean tides; hot desert breezes, sand in my coat and under my paws. A full, brilliant moon.

Home. Somehow, in the pit of me, right next to the whimpering toddler, I know that's Jørn. A place I've only seen in holos, only experienced in training memories, a place I'm meant to care about, but don't.

Psionic schisms are strange things. It's like standing on the edge of a crater with your dad on the other side. He's talking to you, but there's a problem with the comms and, while you can see his mouth move, you can't make out the words. Except all of that is in your own brain.

There's a schism forming now, a split right down the middle of my psyche, and there... There is the creeping dark reaching from the depths, trying to take over part of my brain, trying to plant something there.

Tension rides through the eter, tightens the bands around my chest, squeezes the flesh of my thighs. You might expect desperation from the dark, but no, what's creeping up on me is cold and hard, rich with the coppery scent of blood and the memory of violence. It has no colour. It is the absence of light, and it draws a whimper from the scared toddler in my gut.

It slips through my shields like they're not there and worms its way into my memories, seeking. Too late, I try to rip it out, to rip *me* from its grip, but it's not holding me anymore, it's *part* of me, in my skin and bones, winding through my muscles, trying to make a home.

Shit. Shit. Shit.

What do I do?

There's no Dude here, no Hunt, just me, Aeotu and the darkness. It sinks deeper.

I retreat, but retreating from yourself isn't that easy. Walls and shields and ditches the width of an ocean, I throw all of it, every single scrap between me and it. It laughs. It. Laughs.

The sound is like flippers rubbing together, like a song underwater. It almost sounds like a million Onahs and h'Rawds wrapped into one – if either of the kin breathed underwater.

Wait.

Kin

Under water.

Water-kin.

Well, shit.

Realisation dawns like a new star, loosening the web's hold.

I rip myself out of its embrace.

There two species of kin aboard *Citlali* – air- and tree-kin – but there's a third species, an aquatic one. They didn't come with us for a couple of reasons; the adults will tell you it's because there wasn't enough liquid water aboard the ship, and while it's true, it's not the real reason. We all know the real reason, even if no one actually says it out loud.

The water-kin were fucking scary.

Ask a tree-kin about their aquatic cousins, then watch them struggle to keep their tail from scooting between their legs and their ears from flattening.

There is a story, something you whisper in the dark with a glow pushed up under your chin. A legend made to scare your friends, one you tell where the adults can't hear, one that causes the tree-kin to shudder, and the air-kin's feathers to rise.

It's a story of the water-kin, how they rose out of Jørn's oceans and wrapped their mind around the world to destroy an entire species. An entire *alien* species. It's a story everyone knows but no one talks about, but there's another version, one where the water-kin didn't just destroy the alien minds, but planted something in them, a command buried deep in their psyches where not even a telepath would find it.

I found the command, or it found me, and now it's wrapped

around my mind, crawling in my veins. Now that I know what it is, the black waves make sense, are familiar in the way Onah is familiar. Not exact but close enough that the shape of it makes sense.

The darkness is a command sphere like nothing I've ever seen. It pulses with a life of its own, with a purpose independent of the minds that created it, thick with fear, pain, and retribution. As complex as it is, as weird, it carries a very simple command, one wrapped around an image of *Them* – the flat-nosed aliens the kin once drove from Jørn, the same ones that built Aeotu.

Kill.

# CHAPTER SIXTEEN

Kill.

Kill, kill, kill. Images of *Them* stabbing me in the brain over and over and over.

The command follows me into sleep, trying to pierce my anima.

In that sleep there is no pain, and the darkness is replaced by a torrent of colour. The colours of Aeotu.

The AI is a dark shape, a shadow within the kaleidoscope dancing under her skin, ever changing. Wild. Bright as a supernova. I'm barely able to look at her. She's waiting for me. Waiting for me to wake, to get up or to acknowledge her, one of those things. Or all of them, it's hard to tell. And while she waits, she's focusing elsewhere, only part of her attention on me. There's a bright vein of emotion, of hope amongst the supernova, a bouncing, joyous explosion, and an answering thrum from somewhere outside, a rush of power so immense I think it could swallow me whole. Burn me to atoms.

Movement. We are moving, I can feel the cold glide of the void against the hull, the fire of stray particles, the shiver of thinspace. Thinspace. I don't know that word, and yet... Hunt whispers inside my skull, equations and physics tumbling through my brain, but they're as alien as the whorls and lines on Aeotu's walls. Still, something clicks, something about engines and distance and how time changes... Faster than light, we're travelling FTL, punching through the fabric of space to defy the laws of the universe. Okay. So we're doing that, but then we were doing that before. Travelling to wherever—

*Sister.* The word flashes in the space between Aeotu and I, but she's not referring to me. An image hovers in the kaleidoscope, a ship that looks exactly like the few glimpses I've had of Aeotu, but different somehow. It takes me a moment to see it, a couple of seconds in which Hunt swarms behind my eyes, highlighting the markings on the other ship's hull.

'Euiva.'

Another image, more of a confused jumble of things. The bright pulse of a sun, the hot scent of a quantum signal. All of it adding up to a destination, a place she knows as well as I know the warmth of Mum's arms.

Aeotu's going home, not just to the constellation of minds but the place where she was made.

To Euiva.

*No. You can't. Danger.* My thought shivers through Aeotu, and I sense her turn, the particles impacting her hull lessening as she slows—

Agony knocks me out of Aeotu's mind, wraps me in a cocoon of acid.

*No, fathead.* Grea in my face, Euiva behind her eyes. *You can't stop us.*

I push her away, gasp as I slam back into my own body. Pain chases my nerves, but there's a warm golden fuzz travelling up my brainstem, chasing it away, spreading relief in his wake.

'Dude.'

The critter hums and snuggles under my chin.

'Where are we?'

'On Aeotu.'

I'm lurching to my feet, adrenalin surging on my blood, fug-armour crawling over my shoulders, up my arms—

Mac stands in the corner, crammed into the small space between hatch and bulkhead like he's trying to merge with it. The shiny black of his armour has receded, leaving his head and chest bare. And I mean *bare*, as in skin. No ship suit, no nothing beneath. Just Mac.

Crap. He's put on muscle since I last saw him as like... him, awkwardly returning my hug before Grea dragged me to our family's stasis unit. He was a big guy already, naturally built as Mum would say, with extra cords of muscle added thanks to his semi-addiction to lifting weights. Grea thought the weight training was stupid, kinda like I did before I wrestled fug-eaten handles and doors that refused to budge. Some time in the last ship-cycle before all of this, I pretended to do the gym thing, always making sure I faced the mirror wall.

He's older now, again that jarring shift in age, the years Aeotu took from me manifesting in this shock to my memories, of looking at all the people I knew and loved and realising that I missed something, that they lived without me.

His jaw is broader, squarer, filled out like all those weights added bone to his face, and his eyes... Sadness radiates from them, a beam hitting me in the chest, reaching in and squeezing my heart, but what's worse is the tiredness, the acceptance in their depths, like he's given up. That reaches right into my anima and makes me want to hide, want to look away. The urge is so intense the tendons in my neck stand out like steelcrete cables, as I fight it.

Dude butts my chin, his fuzz warming my muscles, washing away the urge and—

'What are you doing, Mac?' I mean, apart from trying to push every bad emotion he has onto me. 'Stop it,' I say, and there's a growl in my voice.

He frowns, and that urge, that desperate hopelessness, intensifies. His eyes are a laser, directing the emotion right past my shields, filling me up with all the shit in his head, like he wants me to feel what he feels, like he's punishing me. But why?

'You did this,' Mac says, and from the way he says it, the images he thrusts into my mind, he's not talking about our current situation. Or at least, not the one we're in right this second.

He presses harder with his mental attack, the muscles in his chest and shoulders straining as if those somehow count. He only wishes.

Mac should know better than to go up against me in an empathic battle. I mean, his ability is weird, a mash of telepathy and empathy with a little bit of something, the kind of thing that the kin and the scientists don't like to talk about, the kind of thing that shouldn't be possible. But he's not a full empath and he's not me.

I take down my shields, let the full force of his psionic blast in, and capture it. Twisting his attack back on him is easy, and kinda mean, but that hopelessness is buried deep in his psyche. If it weren't deeply rooted, if it didn't have the sense of age, or being so much a part of him, it'd make me angry. Angry that he's given up, angry that maybe he tried so hard and failed, over and over again, that the effort burnt him out, turned my best friend into a husk of what he was. But all of that anger is buried, smothered under sorrow and pain, things almost as bad as the despair wracking him now.

At least he has determination on his side, even if that determination is to blame me for… whatever it is he's blaming me for.

Usually, I'd wrap all of his emotion up in a sticky ball of crap and fire it back at him, but I can't. Just. Can't.

Dude hums, his gold wrapping around my mind, burrowing a hole through my sorrow to the burning core of anger beneath.

Yeah. Yeah, that's it. I let it fill me, gather it in my hands, a molten mass of anger, of rage. There's pain in there too, the kind that stokes fury, makes it stronger. The kind that swallows me whenever I think of the look on Jim Engineer's face.

I don't just throw it at Mac, I follow it in and hammer it home, spreading it through his brain.

He rocks back on his heels, like I smashed him in the face with a hover sled, which I guess I did. Surprise blooms in the air, widens his eyes makes his jaw drop.

The laser beam of hopeless is obliterated. I'm on my feet, punching Mac in the chest with a fug-tipped fist a second later, sending him rocking back into the bulkhead again.

'Not nice, Mac.' The memory of Grea saying the same thing

echoes in my head, makes my gut twist.

He's looking at me, that dumbfounded expression still stamped on his face, but not for long. That anger I planted is there, glowing in his eyes. He pushes back. 'Don't push me, midget.'

I stand straight, and yeah, maybe I'm reaching a little, stretching my calves and spine as far as they'll go, making myself as tall as possible without standing on tip toe. Mac still towers over me, but I don't have to tilt my head to look him in the eye. 'At least I don't have to turn sideways to squeeze through a hatch.'

A glower, Mac's dark brows meeting over his nose, and then... and then... 'What?'

'You know, 'cause your shoulders are so big you have to...' I step back and mime twisting sideways and sliding through a doorway. 'To get through the door.'

Silence. Mac's glower easing, the anger fading away to... 'That's stupid,' he says.

I shrug. 'Hey, it's not my fault it's true.'

'I do *not* need to turn sideways to get through a door.'

I spread my arms, half-squinting like I'm measuring his shoulders. 'I don't know, man. I mean, I'd really need a doorway to measure it against, but from looking...'

Mac grunts and crosses his arms, making the muscles under the dark bronze of his skin bunch in interesting ways. 'You're full of it, Darzi.'

'I know, but at least I look good, right?' The grin is a little forced, coloured by the vestiges of Mac's hopelessness. It easier to pretend it's not there and project other, hotter emotions to counter the effects.

'Hmm.' Mac's looking at me, and some of what I'm projecting is in his eyes, mixed in with other emotions. Confusion is at the front, backed up by a hot, uncomfortable feeling I'm not prepared to name.

I can name the acknowledgement though, right at the back. It swims between us. He knows what I'm doing, what I've done, and I can't help but tense, the beginnings of dread building at the base of my skull. Mac's always been a private person and never liked what I can do, how I can reach in and manipulate people.

He's never said anything, but then he's never had to. Mac isn't exactly shy about sharing his feelings, and knows, in the way only someone with a little bit of empathy can, how to make them known.

'Thanks,' he says. Appreciation rises, a bright yellow fog threading through the air.

I nod. On my shoulder, Dude hums.

'Where's your critter?' I gesture at his shoulder.

'My what?'

'The critter, you know, the little guy that was with you before. The one...' I trail off. I don't want to say 'controlling you', don't want to give the hopelessness something to cling to. Mac's face hardens, and I know I've stuffed shit up, that I probably shouldn't have asked that, but...

'It wasn't a critter, and it's dead.'

'Oh.' I wait a beat, not having to imagine what it would be like if Dude died, seeing none of that grief clinging to Mac. 'What was it?'

'Xin—' He catches himself, makes a face and I'm pretty sure it's because of the blank look on mine. 'It's made of stuff similar to the viyu, the fug as you call it.'

'If it's not a critter, then why does it…?'

'Look like one?' His expression changes, becomes still and dark, despair rising around his ankles. And just like that the moment of happiness, of anger I forced on him, is gone. He points at Dude. 'Probably because of that. Of you.'

Of me. I don't quite get that, what Dude or I have to do with Mac's critter thing.

He turns away. 'Aeotu will send me a new one soon,' he says.

'Why?'

'To replace the old one.'

'But why do you need it? I mean...'

'I'm not like you, Kuma.' The words are quiet, sad. The

hopelessness is rising again, swallowing the anger I'd laid over it. I try to smother it, to emote harder, but no matter how much red and yellow I force into the eter, the dark tide beats against it. There's a force behind it, an intelligence. Mac. Mac is beating back my emote, grabbing hold of the hopelessness and pulling it around him, pushing me out.

'I'm not like you, Kuma.' He says it again, and it's as if the words are a shield or trigger or something, cause all of sudden the darkness has taken over. Shredded the joy and laughter like a hand through mist. 'I wasn't the first Jørgen Aeotu came for.' Memories flood the space, of bodies wrapped in fug, of moans and screams. 'I wasn't even the second.' There, amongst the fug, a familiar face with Mac's almond eyes and dark slashing brows, but older and softer, her jaw a fine, heart-shaped point. Mac's mum.

It's like when I first woke, all that time ago, of slipping into Mum's dream, the scent of burning flesh and the sharp pain as spikes erupted from my chest in a shower of blood. Except it's Mac's mum I'm watching, and while there are no fug-spikes exploding from her chest, she's still screaming, and there's blood running down her chin and—

The memory cuts off, leaving me staring at Mac, at the pain in his eyes.

'Aeotu wanted to make more of...' He gestures at me. 'You. You gave her something, filled a hole in her psyche, but then you were in the escape pod and gone, so she tried to find it with someone else. Except she can't communicate with all of us.'

Mac crosses his arms. 'It needs something specific, something you and Grea have, but most of *us* don't.' A new vision springs to life, of faces I know, of friends, of people I knew by name, that I worked with and played with and ducked chores with. Old, young. A double handful standing in the room with us, staring at me with the same hopelessness in Mac's eyes.

I swallow.

'Are they...?' I can't bring myself to say the word.

'Dead?' Mac says it for me, plucks it out of the ether like it's something he does all the time. That thought freezes my insides. 'Some of them.' A handful of the faces fade, not disappearing, just fading, becoming translucent and grey, ghosts in the eter. 'Others aren't so lucky.'

The vision changes again, the faces changing, the bodies distorting, growing too-heavy limbs and holes in places that shouldn't have them. There are tendrils coming out one boy's head, replacing his hands, sprouting from his back, reminding me of Grea, stalking through the darkness with a cloak of viyusa. Only he isn't moving and his eyes... I reach, push through the darkness and latch onto the essence of him.

Cold reaches back, runs up my arm and runs for my brain. It's not him, not the boy I remember, the sensation is barely even Jørgen. There's no thought there, no intelligence, no memory, just... just...

*Brother.*

*Aeotu.* I breathe her name, the sound of it rising on the eter.

A pulse, warm, welcoming.

I thrust her away. Turn to Mac.

'What happened to them?'

Sadness, anima-deep, climbs up his feet, encasing him in another kind of armour. 'They're not empaths. Aeotu couldn't talk to them like she can us, and so...' He shrugs. 'She tried to fix it, but didn't know what she was doing.'

'But why? Why...' I gesture down at myself, at Mac, at the armour crawling over our skins.

'I don't know.' Tiredness rolls off Mac, is in the droop of his shoulders. 'I don't know, Kuma. She doesn't speak to me, she tries and...' He shrugs. 'I can feel her sometimes, but it's strange, half-heard, like it's through a veil or a bad comm connection. The xin help, but...' He shrugs again.

'You have to stand on your head.' The words are out before I realise how ridiculous they sound, and the look on Mac's face reinforces that. I feel the blush rising up my neck. 'Psionically, you kind of have to... twist? It's strange, but once you get it—'

'I can't get it. I told you, I'm not like you, I can't do the same things.'

'But you're—'

'Weird? Different? That I'd be the only telekinetic *ever*, if only the kin and psy-researchers admitted it was a thing?' He leans back. 'Some kinds of different aren't all they're cracked up to be, Kuma. You should know that.'

'What's that mean?'

Mac's jaw gets tight, and he looks away, but not before his eyes travel down my chest, lingering there for a second. 'Just...' Words trail off, and the emotion that rolls off of him... Confusion, the same nervous flutter in Mac's chest that I feel in mine when I look at him, and buried beneath it all, embarrassment. The embarrassment comes wrapped around a jumbled image of Grea and me, with my face on her curves.

It's... wrong. It's a betrayal, a slap in the face from my best friend.

It's enough to force me back a step, and then two. I slam shields in place, but the sticky pink of his emotion has its fingers in me, digs deep into the heart of me where the new, unsure feelings live. Turns them brown and putrid, makes my chest constrict and my heart lodge painfully in my throat.

Somewhere distant, Grea is a firestorm rising in the eter. Anger and outrage rush before her, and a little bit of it infects me. Shoves the putrid emotion away and covers it in flame.

On my shoulder, Dude growls.

Mac's still looking away, face still stone, but there's a line between his brows, a quiver to his lip that might be regret.

Silence rolls between us.

I need to go, need to—

The bulkheads explode, and there's only time to react. Viyusa fills the room, giant, angry vines, the heat of Grea's fury riding before them, turning the ends into spears.

# CHAPTER SEVENTEEN

We're crashing through bulkheads, pounding down corridors, skidding around corners. Throwing ourselves through walls of grey-green that snap shut on our heels. There's no rest, no reprieve, no time to breathe. There's just the viyusa hunting us, steaming through the Aeotu like a tide. We tried fighting it, tried slashing and ripping through the vines. It worked for a minute, we gained ground, cleared the room, and for handful of heartbeats, with our hands on our knees and our lungs working overtime, we thought we'd won.

No such luck.

The viyusa came back harder, the tips of it glowing, dripping heat like it was some kind of acid. Aeotu screamed. *Screamed* in my head, in pain, and the fug screamed with her, that piecing, brain-shredding sound it made. Only the fug-armour kept me on my feet and only Dude kept me moving. Mac wasn't so lucky. Without his xin, he crumbled, hitting the deck, a hundred kilos of muscle and bone.

Fug-armour gave me the strength to pick him, to throw him over my shoulder and run.

I'd stopped when Mac started to move on his own, propped him up against a half-eaten bulkhead when I thought it was safe, waited for him to get his feet back. That was the second time we fought the fug, the last one too. One moment I was trying to figure out what was happening, was trying to find Grea amongst the mess of anger, thought I was getting somewhere. And then the anger was on us, and so was the viyusa.

We didn't fight for as long, couldn't. The red just kept coming. Again and again and again, rolling on the tide of anger.

And so we ran again, and we're still running, and I'm pretty sure that soon enough we're going to run out of ship.

My breath's coming in pants. 'We have... to get out... of here.'

*I know.* Mac's voice sounds in my head, only a trace of breathlessness in his mind, even though he's sweating just as much as me, lungs working just as hard. The benefits of being a telepath, or maybe it's practise. Does Mac do a lot of running from viyusa? There's no panic coming off him, no emotion at all. *Ahead.* An image forms in my brain, of a bulkhead and a symbol I remember from the airlock.

'That's... vacuum.'

There's no answer to that, save perhaps a brief spike of acknowledgment.

I want to object, to tell Mac he can't survive vacuum with only half of his armour, but my muscles need the oxygen for running, and surely Mac knows... Surely.

Viyusa snapping on our heels, and there's the bulkhead, a great section of it already becoming translucent, snapping back, and then we're through and there's the airlock, and we're rushing through that too. And Mac... Mac's still shirtless and faceplateless, and my HUD's throwing up warnings, highlighting the final airlock in bright screaming red as his hand smashes against the release.

'Mac!' I'm yelling it, and he's looking at me with this scared expression in his eyes, but there's calm there too, a deep-seated exhaustion that drags at my bones just acknowledging it.

I'm across the airlock, hands on his shoulders, not sure what I'm doing but all-too-sure that I can't let my best friend die. That I *won't* let him die. I'm grabbing at his fug-armour, hands and mind, digging fingers in, pulling and yanking, twisting my psyche and slipping through the threads of the world, screaming.

I'm not sure who I'm screaming at. At Aeotu, at Grea, at the fug. Just screaming, fear and desperation giving my voice power, turning my thoughts into hooks. There's a tingle on the edge of my consciousness, something that feels like Aeotu, but not. More like a shadow of her, of the lightning in the fug. It hears me, turns in my direction and for a moment, for a moment there is hope, there is movement, fug-armour shifting under my physical hands, reaching for Mac's shoulders—

The HUD is blaring in my ears, filling my vision with red. Temperature not just dropping, but gone, sucked into space with the atmosphere. With us.

Mac is boiling. Moisture sucked from his eyes, his mouth opening on a breath that isn't there and—

Dude. Leaping from my shoulder, landing on Mac's. Talons extended, a flash of blood, frozen in the instant it breaks skin.

Fug flowing up my arms, over my hands, following Dude. Spreading outward from his paws, covering Mac's chest, his shoulders, encasing his face. Three heartbeats, and Mac is floating in my arms, safe from the vacuum, from the killing void. But was it fast enough? Is he—

His hands are on my arms, fingers gripping. Relief floods through me.

He's all right.

*I'm all right*, he says. His relief echoes mine, except... There's a small piece of darkness floating on the blue-green of his relief, a worm wriggling through the endorphin rush. It makes my heart cold, speaks of endings and endless sleep, speaks to the emotion in me, the one that took hold as I was floating in the stasis unit, waiting for the end.

I don't want to feel that, don't want to see it. Don't like the memories it stirs, of floating in the stasis unit, letting the cold take me.

I turn away.

We're in the void, floating outside Aeotu. Just us, and our fug.

The expulsion of atmosphere has pushed us away from the hull, and we're still moving. There's nothing out here to slow us down, nothing to stop us from floating forever, farther and farther from the only oxygen in a hundred parsecs.

The HUD is calculating distance and velocity, the time we have left to live. It's not much. All we have is the oxygen trapped in our armour. Minutes-worth. Maybe, if we're lucky. It might have been more, but Mac lost all of his and some of mine is now keeping Mac alive.

If we keep travelling like this, we're screwed. In a regular EVA suit there'd be a tether or a thrusters, or *something* to keep us from drifting forever. We might already be screwed, what with the lack of thrusters and—

A jolt, like my shoulder blades being ripped out of my back, spread open and—

Pain, ripping through my muscles. Liquid heat in my bones, digging into my spine. I can't scream. There's no breath, my lungs are frozen and every nerve in my body is too busy being fried for such a petty thing as screaming.

Mac's yelling in my head, but the words are drowned beneath pain and horror, 'cause I can see what's happening. Hunt is in my brain, has taken over the armour, and is showing me, in minute detail, what it's doing. Fug peeling away from my skin, driving spikes into my back, can see blood and bone. Frozen in the instant it spurts forth. It's over in nano-seconds. Barely long enough for the void to take my marrow and make it ice, but it feels like hours. And then it's done, the pain over, fug shifting over my back, still forming new protrusions, rearranging itself.

Hunt is still in my head, embedded in my brain, nestled next to a new perception, new muscles, new nerves, new bones that stretch and flex, that gather power. My HUD is going dark, all the heat in my body drawing up from my toes to the spot between my shoulder blades. Gathering there, getting hot. Hunt is behind my eyes, seeing through them, taking over as the last of the HUD's glow fades, leaving me staring at the dark. Except it's not dark, not for Hunt. For Hunt, it's clear as day, another HUD printed on the back of my eyeballs.

Mac has stopped yelling, his mental voice no longer ringing in my head, but he's still talking to me. I have the vague sense of the words, of him asking me if I'm okay, what's happening. Worry and fear colour him a dirty brown, but there's no space to answer, no time. There's just Hunt and the new form on my back. Not quite a limb, not quite an organ, just... a small sun between my shoulder blades.

There's purpose in Hunt's presence, in the way the miniature sun keeps drawing all the energy from my body, concentrating it. There's a moment, a brief pause, a sense of accomplishment, a tightening of the connection between Mac and I, and I finally understand what the fug has done.

The sun explodes.

We're shooting across the void, the lines and whorls of Aeotu's hull getting bigger and bigger until they're the size of my head and then my torso and then they're dwarfing me and the rough texture of the metal-stone is all I can see.

I don't know how fast we're going, don't know how to stop, but it's got to be at least as fast as we were expelled into space. Faster maybe. Without the HUD there's no way to know, and I don't want to find out by going splat on Aeotu's skin.

Just as the texture of the hull is starting to look like dunes instead of pebbles, the supernova stops. Another, small explosion goes off behind my ribs. We spin, and now we're staring out at the void, except it's not a void anymore. I only notice the explosion on the other side of my body, another mini sun going off under my ribs, because we stop spinning, and I can stare at the not-void.

It's not a not-void, it's just space, space filled not with the dark emptiness of the cold between stars, but with the giant grey-black ball of a planet, the light of a sun blazing off a dozen tiny orbiting moons, and the smooth, cylindrical lines of the kind of satellite that isn't molten rock getting spewed into space. It's what's around the satellite though that stuns my brain, makes it difficult to think.

The supernova fires one last time, slowing us before we pancake on the hull. My brain is still ringing with the sight of the satellite, with the cold in my bones and the memory of my body being ripped apart. It's Mac who gets us across the hull, Hunt who whispers where to go. Mac's still in my head, I sense him following Hunt's directions, can sense the freaked-out wonder as the awareness reaches through me and into him. Can sense too, that there's not much time left, not much oxygen.

I'm still stuck on what I'm seeing.

There's an airlock. We're dropping into a hole in the hull, then the hull's snapping shut over us and Mac's twisting me about, pointing my feet at the deck before the gravity kicks in.

Fug peels back, flows down Mac's arms, back to me. Dude's on my shoulder and there's that wave of gold, pushing back the unreality.

'Kuma, come on.' Mac's yanking on my arm, pulling me to another hatch.

I stare at him, feet not moving. 'Did you see that?'

'We don't have time for this, Kuma. We have to get—' He yanks again.

I yank back, pulling him off his feet. 'Did you see *that*?' I'm pointing at the bulkhead, I'd point straight through if I could, would shoot a laser straight from my finger to the cluster of ships orbiting the satellite.

His face is pale, and there's a little too much white around the brown of his eyes. 'Kuma—'

'Did. You. See. It?'

There's a moment, a pause in which Mac turns to stone. Then he nods.

'Okay.' A deep breath in. Another one out. 'Okay,' I say again, and nod. So I wasn't crazy, all of that, all the floating husks that looked just like Aeotu... they were there. I hadn't been the only one to see them.

Dude's still swamping my psyche with gold, but it's a little more frantic now, and little more urgent. My HUD's still dark, and my bones cold. I figure my stomach is going to start gnawing at my backbone any minute, once it unfreezes enough to remember what hunger is.

There's no sound, but the raw anger of the viyusa is getting bigger in my mind.

We run, Mac following me, me following the not-so-gentle tug of Hunt in my gut. Somewhere along the way, things start to look familiar, and then we're pounding across the docking tube from Aeotu to *Citlali*.

A dark grey-green shape flies out of the shadows, whizzing past my face. I turn just enough to see a not-critter, a xin, attach itself to Mac's shoulder, to witness the armour flowing over his face before we burst through the airlock and into a battlefield.

# CHAPTER EIGHTEEN

I've only seen a battlefield in training memories, felt the heat of a Jøran desert, the rumble of shuttles flying overhead and the shredded remains of kin and humans staining the sand red.

This is different. Not because it's in the middle of the Attrium, with the broken remnants of the giant plassteel dome overhead and the trunk of one of Aeotu's grappling cables erupting through deck. And not because the combatants are encased in envirosuits, helmets jammed over round and triangular heads alike. No, it's got nothing to do with that.

In the training memory, guns spat lances of energy, searing the flesh they didn't blow away, filling the air with the smell of cooking meat. Here, there's fire, the sharp beam of Franken-lasers, but instead of smoking flesh, there's the high-pitched screaming of fug, the fine grey of dead nanites saturating the atmosphere in little puffs of dust.

Grey-green and red alike, fighting, tearing. Humans and kin standing shoulder-to-shoulder, qwan riding on rucnarts, swarms of plasform-wrapped critters arrayed before them, and in my brain... Shards of ice and fire, daggers and claws and teeth, ripping at the eter, flowing along lines of yellow-gold, following it through the threads of the universe and sinking into fug.

And above it all, hovering just on the edge of my consciousness, is Grea.

*Kuma!* The word is mental is much as physical. I have a split second to turn, to slip back into the real world and see Mac, arms outstretched, like he's throwing something, before a wall of force knocks me off my feet.

My head hits the deck, rattles my brain. Stars burst in my vision. It's hard to tell which is the eter and which is real. Time slows, is molasses. In the eter there are days in which to see the bomb exploding over Mac, the thin plassteel dome expanding, the fire burst from inside pushing sharp, shining fragments of shit into the atmosphere. Tiny volcanos of blood erupt on Mac's chest, embed themselves in the space where I was standing.

Fear. Pain. They spew from Mac as he flies backward, the bomb's shockwave rippling his flesh.

Hunt is there, not just in my gut, but with me in the eter. A flat-faced sentinel at my back. Solid. Calm. Relentless.

Fug-armour is flowing over my body, the thrusters on my back drawing the heat from my bones even as new protrusions form over my arms, an incandescent vein throbbing over my shoulders to my forearms. The fug-blades *snick* out over my knuckles, but instead of the sharp grey-green, they're glowing yellow-white, heat coming off them in waves.

And then I'm racing across the deck, throwing myself into the fray. Hacking and slashing, left and right, not even sure what I'm slashing at, *who* I'm slashing at. Hunt has hold of my brain. On my shoulder, the golden web of Dude's control thrums under my skin, but Hunt isn't listening.

Not to me at least. I can hear Aeotu behind Hunt, not actual words but a buzz, and the sickness of before… It fills her up, makes me want to puke just touching it.

There's a wall of muscle on my left, and I'm on the deck rolling backward, finding my feet and coming up and under the sweep of h'Lott's forearms, dancing out of her reach. Then I'm slashing, but not at h'Lott, or the viyu rising out of the floor, thick spiky tendrils coming to my defence, tangling in the rucnart's legs. No, I'm slashing at a fist-sized sphere hurtling through the vacuum, and then another and another. They shatter under my blades, the spheres breaking apart, the contents a smoking ruin before it has a chance to bleed.

There are more traces of gold flying through the battle, critters in plasform bubbles defying gravity, hunting down the grey-green, smashing into it, kamikaze-style. Exploding on impact. The viyu seems to absorb it, the parts that do turning grey, crumbling to dust, the rest of it carrying on and then... Have you ever seen biopoison creep up a grow wall, seen the green leaves turn brown, watched them wither and die? That's what this is. Gold runs through the viyu like blood, traces of it gleaming in the light of Franken-throwers, and with every explosion, every new injection of poison Aeotu gets sicker.

I never thought of gold as a bad colour, you always think of red that way, or black or any of the hundred oozy, rotten shades of dank green and rank orange, but never gold. Now though... Now it makes my skin crawl, my stomach curdle. The viyu doesn't scream, not like it does when you hit it with flame, or when the viyusa digs in. Nope, it kind of whimpers as sickness rolls off it in waves of puke-yellow.

Hunt twists me out of the way as another critter bomb explodes at my feet. I'm leaping high, pulling fug-feet up to my chest, watching as some of that gold splatters against me.

Hunt keeps moving, keeps twisting and slashing, but there are warnings going off on the HUD, and that sickness? It's creeping up my toes, through my veins. My toes goes first, talons crumbling as I hit the deck, gold wrapping itself around my ankles, climbing higher— Dude's off my shoulder, scrambling down my body. All I can do is watch, heart in throat, wanting to scream "No".

Red is there before Dude, the viyusa erupting out of the deck, clamping me in place, jerking me off my feet. Hunt tries to keep fighting, blades swinging, but we're on the floor.

I'm expecting fire, expecting the viyusa to burn, to devour Dude. I'm not expecting it to chase the gold, to pass over the fuzzbutt like he's not there, even when the critter sinks teeth, talons and barbed tail into it. The gold is gone, eaten by the red, and my toes are rebuilding themselves, absorbing the red just like the inert fug.

I'm still staring at it when darkness explodes in the middle of the ruined Attrium, fire writhing around it.

Everything stops.

Guns, growls, the kins' icy daggers. Just. Stops.

The darkness unfurls, standing in a smooth, graceful motion, its fire becoming long tendrils of red, fanning around its feet like a cape. Dragging on the ground. At its edges, the fug, both red and green, rolls back, leaving a half-metre of scarred and broken deck in its wake.

The only thing that dares approach are the critter balls and they're swatted out of the air like bugs.

Grea stands in the midst of it, the focal point of all that darkness, all that fire. Purpose bleeds through the barrier between eter and the physical, staining the atmosphere a shining bronze.

She's not wearing a mask. The harsh glow of the battle plays across her face in harsh shadow and violent orange highlights, washing out her complexion, making the sharp lines of her cheekbones and the hollows of her cheeks stand out in stark relief. She's changed again since I last saw her, grown taller, gotten older, and I wonder how long she kept me in the dark place, wracking my body with pain.

*Not long, little brother.* Her eyes find mine, boring through my faceplate. *Euiva needed an older body for what comes next.* Pain echoes through the words, the memory of it laced with determination.

Is it my heart that chills or Aeotu's? It's not Hunt's, although there's a new whirring in the depths of my brain, calculations, vectors, numbers, strategies piling up in its consciousness, a sense of impending danger.

Why would Aeotu be afraid? And why would Euiva need Grea to be physically older?

The fear that shivers under my skin is all mine. Other emotions, though, the wonder, the joy and shock. Those are not mine. Those are carried on the colours of Mum and Dad's minds, of Mac's dad and the white/black of Onah. They splash against my back, trying to thaw that shiver, almost succeeding.

'Grea?' Mum's voice comes through my comms, echoing in my helmet.

I doubt Grea can hear her, not in vacuum, without comms to bridge vacuum. Of course, nothing's ever impossible.

Grea turns, facing Mum, a smile lighting her face, and I guess, if Grea's face still isn't a frozen block of flesh, if she's somehow immune to the vacuum, then hearing Mum despite the lack of comms isn't that far of a stretch.

Grea's mouth moves. There's no air, not even enough for her breath to frost, and yet... 'Hi Mum. Sorry about not coming to find you, but I had to do something.'

It's Dad's turn now. He clumps forward, not quite as graceful in his envirosuit as he usually is. 'Baby, what's going on?'

'I have to go, Dad, there's not much time, but Kuma knows, ask him.' She turns away, the red closing in tight around her, darkness following, but she pauses a moment before she's swallowed by it, and smiles at Dad. 'It's okay,' she says. 'We'll be done soon, but you should go now.'

There's a thud, a kind of muffled explosion, and then she's gone, disappeared through a new hole in the deck.

I'm over the edge of it, peering at the faint blue shimmer of emergency bulkheads lighting up the tunnel, my HUD scanning the hole. Ten decks, Grea just bored her way through *all* of *Citlali's* decks, not just one or two, and she did it like it was nothing, or like she was made of the same stuff as Aeotu's grappling cables.

I jump in after her. It's not an action I think about, and the moment my feet leave the deck I wonder if my fug-self can soak the damage, if falling forty-eight metres is the same as nine, or if I'm going to wind up with broken legs and my spine lodged in my brain. Probably something I should have figured out before the leap.

I have a nano-second to regret the impulse, and then warmth flares on my back. The thrusters.

Hunt is running numbers in the back of my brain. According to it and the HUD, there's enough power in them to prevent me from breaking every bone in my body. Armour is shifting, flowing from my torso and arms to my legs, just in case.

"Just in case" doesn't inspire confidence in Hunt's calculations.

Still. I only have seconds to regret my decision.

There's a jolt as I pass through the emergency bulkhead, an electric, biting ripple that starts in my toes and surges up my body, and then air is rushing past my face, lifting my hair. The armour is bulked around my lower body, just the thrusters attached to my back and a thin skeleton around my face, enough to support the HUD.

Numbers are counting down. And there's the bottom of the shaft, highlighted in red and yellow. The thrusters are firing, slowing my descent, but the numbers on my HUD are still high, still make my gut clench with the expectation of pain, even as they leach all the energy from my bones. Impact comes both sooner and later than I expect. The deck meets my feet in slow-motion, my knees bending, force rushing up my legs, making the armour ripple. Warnings are screaming, force meters red to rival the emergency lights, but there's no pain. No *crunch* of bones, no tear of muscles. Just fug, cracking with a wet *scrittch*, turning grey, crumbing to dust as the nanites die.

Weight falls off my back, the thrusters joining the pile of dead fug at my feet.

I follow it, collapsing to the cold deck, exhaustion turning my bones to steelcrete, my muscles to biogel, pulling my eyes closed. It's cold, I know it's cold because icicles are forming in my nose, clogging up my airways, but I can't summon the energy to get up.

Maybe jumping after Grea wasn't such a good idea.

*Grea.* I reach for her. She's ahead of me, racing down the corridor, darkness and viyusa propelling her faster than any human can move on their own.

I feel her stop, feel her turn and look down the corridor, straight through the curve of the bulkhead. For a moment it's as if she's standing right there, the tendrils of viyusa brushing against my sides, skittering away from my armour like it hurts.

She hesitates, leans forward, and warmth springs in my chest – she's coming back for me – but then someone else tugs at her psyche. It's faint, weak, but insistent, powerful with urgency, with desperation.

Grea turns away, purpose driving her from me.

*Grea!* My own desperation, the first stirrings of fear, colour the call.

My twin, my other half, ignores it. And then she's gone. Just. Gone.

Alone. Cold.

I should be used to it, should have inured myself to the creeping chill, to the numbness as ice forms in my blood, slows my heart, makes it hard to remember why I'm here. And yet… and yet this is different, this is a dagger ripping my heart in two. This is a piece of myself gone. Lost. Torn away. Stolen.

This is unacceptable.

*Brother.*

Aeotu crouches beside me, the dark, sleek shadow looking so much like Mac in his armour, except it's not him. The kaleidoscope dances under Aeotu's skin, purple, green, blue, the colours I have no names for, no ability to describe, twisting and turning. Whorls and lines sucking me in, talking to me, to Hunt. Sharing secrets and whispering lies. Endless. Infinite. I can see the void in her skin, the infinite cold of FTL, the possibility of the universe.

*Brother.* She reaches into my back, through flesh and bone and fug, her sleek, talon-like fingers wrapping around my heart. And I realise, as those deadly claws pierce the muscle, that she used the male pronoun. *Up.* Lightning, the kaleidoscope jumpstarting my heart, pumping energy into my blood, my bones melting, my marrow throbbing.

I'm on my feet. Fug is flowing over my flesh, the grey-green rippled with the yellow of the neo-critters, encasing my feet, my knees, hiding the gold of Jørgen-me under the armour of the new me. The one with claws that tear into steelcrete, with a miniature sun on his back and blades sheathed in his arms. That Kuma, the one tearing down the corridor, mind stretching ahead, finding Grea, slipping into her mind, pushing past the shock, sharing her eyes as she powers up the shuttle. Sensing the other, Euiva, as it whispers in Grea's ear.

*Don't.* The word is mine.

*I have to.* There is a world behind that response, centuries of loneliness and pain, of floating in the void, an abandoned hull leaking atmosphere. Of emotions that bubble up from deep within, as alien as the dark swirl of colour it rises out of, as powerful as a sun.

*Sister.* Aeotu speaks through me, her voice reaching through the connection that is Kuma/Grea to speak to the thing on the other side.

Grea jerks, tries to rip herself away, but I'm holding tight. *It can't have you,* I say.

A denial, violent, angry. It reaches through Grea like Aeotu reaches through me. Hooks into the connection. Cold. Hard.

Aeotu screams.

I scream with her.

Grea rips away. Is gone.

I skid through the shuttle bay doors on my knees, pain stealing my coordination. The doors snap closed. Lights are flashing, a hazard holo is in my face. The sleek, egg-shape of the shuttle is rising, hovering over the deck before it turns, thrusters firing white hot, the hover jets creating a mini tornado, sweeping the crumbled remnants of deck and scaffolding.

The outer doors open. The little atmosphere in the hangar is sucked into space, taking me with it.

I flip on my belly, ram claws the length of my forearm into the deck, picture hooks forming on the ends, holding me in place even as the rush of atmosphere lifts my body from the deck.

The shuttle is pointed at the outer airlock, toward the dark tunnel of the ice hull.

*Grea.* I try again.

Euiva encases my twin; my call bounces off.

Thrusters fire.

The shuttle is gone.

# CHAPTER NINETEEN

Mum's standing in the shuttle bay looking like Grea took the shuttle and smacked her in the face. Dad's next to her, looking the same and Onah...

Honestly, I never really thought the air-kin cared about Grea that much. I mean, he's always cared about me, in his own way, but the emotion coming off him now...

I double-down on my shields. There's too much emotion in the air and not enough of me left to care.

Or maybe there's too much of me left. Too much raw skin and heartache, too much feeling. I want to explode out of my flesh, want to run through *Citlali's* corridors screaming. I've done so much, so much has been done to me, that this part, the part where I get to fall into my parents' arms and go to sleep beside my twin, it should be easy. And I guess it would be, if I got it at all.

But all I can see is Grea gunning the shuttle, all I can feel is that slimy, creeping madness looking out of her eyes, using her voice and leaving me behind.

Always leaving me behind.

*Brother.*

I ignore it, tighten my shields, give them forcefields and coat them in lava.

*Brother.*

*No.* I twist the forcefield, turn it into a beam of light and shoot it at the kaleidoscope on the edge of my eter.

Except it's not coming through the eter, not entirely.

The umbilicus pulses with Aeotu's presence. Hunt is behind her, and there is urgency in its touch, pushing Aeotu forward.

*Brother. Danger.* Darkness rolls behind her, carrying words and impressions that make my eyes cross and slip over my brain without touching it. Things too alien for me to comprehend.

Hunt though... Hunt gobbles it up, its processors whirring, spinning images in my brain, little bits and pieces that don't make sense. Strange fragments of tubes and vines that remind me of fug, if fug were smooth and round, with sharp edges and—

The images *SNAP* together, forming a whole that makes my heart sink. 'The FTL engines.'

Dad turns. 'What about them?'

Aeotu/Hunt are still speaking, shoving more and more information at me. And Old Terra help us, it's coming together and that sinking feeling, it doesn't encompass what Grea has done, what she's left us with. What she's planning.

But why? Why does she want to blow up *Citlali*?

*Why?* I send the thought winging through the void, chasing after my twin. There's no answer, and I wish there were, something to wipe away the horror taking over my anima.

'Kuma?' Hands on my shoulders, jerking me around, pulling me face-to-forehead with Dad. 'Kuma,' he says again. 'What about the engines?'

There's fear in his voice, in his grip; knowledge too, an awful kind of inevitability.

Somehow, some way, Dad already knows what Aeotu is telling me, what the AI has only just discovered.

'How?' I ask him. 'How do you know what she did?'

It's an interesting thing when Dad pales. The blood leaves his skin, takes the warm, rosy flush out of his cheeks, leaves his lips the colour of death and turns the flesh under his eyes the colour of old blood. His fingers might as well be bone digging into my biceps, trying to scoop out the marrow in my bones.

'It was Grea.' The statement is soft. Dad's looking at me, but his gaze is clouded by the images behind his eyes, and his aura... I've never seen one break like that, split right down the middle and collapse. Heartbreak. You learn something new every day, I just wish I didn't have to learn it from Dad.

Over his shoulder, Mum's aura is the same. Dark and split.

Dad shakes himself. 'The FTL engines have been rigged to overload. We don't know how, some kind of amalgamation of *Their* tech and ours.'

'You thought it was me.' It's an accusation. Hurt is blooming in my chest, you wouldn't think there was room, or that I'd be used to it, but there's a Grea-sized hole in my anima now. Plenty of room for other things.

Dad doesn't answer with words, his eyes tell it all, catching on Dude perched on my shoulder, sliding off the fug.

I step back.

There's resistance, just a tiny bit, Dad's grip tightening before he lets go, hands dropping to his sides. Still not looking at me.

'Yeah. The kid with the strange appendages must be the one planning to blow up the home he tried to save.'

'Kuma...' Mum steps up beside Dad. I wait for her to say something, to find the words to soothe the hurt bits, the way mums do. She just stares at me.

It's my turn to look away. I want to keep looking, to force them to *see* me, not the fug crawling over my body, but that just makes the hurt boil, makes it harder to hold in the words that want to spew from my mouth, the ones that'll hurt. I'll make sure they hurt, load them up with all the shit inside and fire them not just at my parents, but at *everyone*; the kind of destructive *emote* that makes people fear me. The kind that sticks inside and doesn't let go, not for a year, not for a month, not for a millennium. The kind that changes an entire species.

The kind the water-kin used against *Them*.

I swallow the urge, step back and turn away. 'I'll go get her, make her stop it.'

*Too late.* Aeotu's voice echoes, not just in my head or through the umbilicus, but in my *ears*.

Mum's looking around, hope wiping away the worry on her brow. 'Core? Is that you?'

*No.*

'It's Aeotu. Core's dead.' The words are mine and they're cold. The fact that Aeotu has found a way into the comms doesn't surprise me, I've heard it before after all, and besides, while Grea's absence has left room for shit, there's none for the alarm I might have felt otherwise. Besides, Mum should know that. She's been trying to resurrect *Citlali's* AI for long enough.

You'd think I was in a graveyard the way the faces around me drain of colour.

Not surprising. First, they're confronted with a son who's not quite Jørgen anymore and then the being who remade him is hijacking their systems and telling them the world is falling down. If that's not bad enough, there's Mac, dropping from the ceiling three decks above like it ain't nothing, all fugged out, faceplate down, whorls and lines moving under his armour.

*It has spread. Cannot save sister—*

'*Citlali.*' That's Mac, translating for Mum before the confusion has thought about crossing her face. 'You have to evacuate.'

Silence.

I'm not sure if it's because they're too busy staring at the dark grey humanoid with Mac's voice, or if they're processing what he just said. I know I am, but for them... For them it's probably both.

In the back of my head I'm remembering another voice, another face, 'stasis separation' ringing in my ears. We all know how that went.

No. Not again.

Mum's saying things about air filters and bio-sponges, all the words adding up to the same thing. They can't. What she really means is 'they won't'. All the junk about pollen counts and oxygen ratios can't cover up the revulsion in her aura. Can't hide the dismay as Mac's faceplate retracts and they see him for the first time. The boy who used to spend so much time in our living room he was practically family.

I'm not listening anymore. I'm cutting myself off from the torrent of emotion filling the shuttle bay and doing what I need to do. What no one else can.

I'm going after Grea.

I'm going to stop her from blowing up Citlali.

# CHAPTER TWENTY

There aren't any more shuttles and the pods we use to make repairs to *Citlali* might get me where I need to go, in about a hundred years.

It's okay though, 'cause I don't need them.

Hunt is in the back of my mind, not saying anything, just there, a beacon guiding me through *Citlali's* ruined corridors, through the gangway connecting it to Aeotu, and deep into the alien ship's bowels.

It's different down here, the bulkheads dark, the patterns carved deeper, sharper. Urgency and danger radiate from them, saturating the air, my blood, making my heart beat harder. From Aeotu or Hunt? I can't tell. All I know is that the vision of Hunt, of the faceless thing on the other side of the umbilicus, is more vibrant down here.

The atmosphere tastes like old sweat and adrenalin, musty and ancient, seeped into the bulkheads over millennia ago.

I can almost see *Them* racing down these stairs, almost feel like I am one of *Them*, fug-feet taking the risers without the awkwardness of my human legs. And now I'm stepping through a doorway, the hatch *snapping* shut behind and it almost feels familiar.

There's no corridor here, just a room. An airlock, the last line of defence if the—

I shake my head. The stuff in my brain is a tangle of numbers and equations, things slipping through Hunt's translation and skidding off my grey-matter. It doesn't matter why this is an airlock, all that matters is the massive, squashed-egg-on-its-side hatch in front of me, and the thing behind it.

My heart's pounding hard, the *SNICK SNICK* of my fug-claws boom in my ears, and I can't get my breath.

The hatch pulses under my hand, the vibration rippling up my arm, beating in time with my heart. Whatever's behind the door is going to change my life, change it in ways that the fug-armour has only hinted at, and I can't help remembering Grea whispering to me in the dark. *'We're going to live forever.'*

I don't want to live forever. That knowledge blooms in my anima, in the very core of me.

I'm gonna live for now though. Got to find a way to get to Grea and out of the mess she's landed us in, and that way is on the other side of the hatch.

I take a step, draw in a breath to fortify my courage, and nod. 'Okay,' I say. 'Let's do this.'

A pulse of acknowledgement, and then the wall snaps back.

The space beyond is cavernous, three decks tall and four times as wide. For a moment, I imagine a half-dozen shuttles crouched on the deck, furred, flat-nosed aliens scurrying between them, carrying tools and dragging hover-sleds laden with cargo, and struggle to know if the imagining is mine or Aeotu's.

The hangar is dark and deserted now, the massive expanse of deck empty but for dust and the metallic sentinel waiting for me on the other side; the only light comes from the corridor and the glow hovering over my shoulder. It's barely enough to make out the thing's feet.

The thought has barely crossed my mind before light floods the space, and I know by the pulse through the umbilicus, that it's Hunt responding to me.

It's huge. A steel grey colossus of metal. The HUD is mapping the... armour? Human-shaped shuttle? Mechanoid? Mech? Whatever it is, the HUD outlines it in white and red and blue.

Eight-point-three-five metres. The *awareness* tells me that a second before my HUD starts popping numbers, readouts and power levels and material scans flying outward from the centre of my vision, cluttering up the sides of the screen.

I ignore them. Numbers and scans can't quite encompass the enormity of the thing before me, can't quite describe the unreality, the coolness, the deep-seated freak-out happening in my chest.

The mech *is* Hunt, and it looks like me. There's no face, no nose, no eyes, just a blank space on the top of its neck. It barely even has a *neck*, the head sloping into the shoulders with a short stump between. No hair. No nothing that would immediately make you sit up and go 'Holy Terra, they turned Kuma into a robot', but somehow... Somehow it looks like me. There's an aura coming off the mech, a sense of identity that wasn't there when I first saw it, was just a nascent glimpse of the future. And now, now its identity radiates off it and... It's me but not.

I take a breath, a big one. There's no time to wonder at it.

Dude chitters, his paw on my ear as he rears up for a better look.

The multi-hued thread connecting the critter to Hunt, pulses.

*Brother. Hurry.*

Aeotu's voice shivers through the air, pushing me forward, reminding me of Grea and the ships outside.

I hurry, fug-feet padding across the deck.

I'm at the mech's feet, the top of its toes coming up to my chest, before I wonder how I get *in*. Do I get in? Aeotu made it sound like I was taking a shuttle, so *in* makes sense but—

Knowledge smacks me in the back of the head, and there's that golden web moving under my skin as Dude takes control of my feet. I'm jogging, feet aiming for a circle carved in the deck before the knowledge finishes sinking in. I'm in the circle and the outside of it is glowing, my HUD picking up the surge of power, and then we're shooting into the air as Dude releases my muscles. It's fast enough to make me wobble, to find myself peering over the edge of the platform as it leaves the deck behind and... Oh shit, I did not expect that.

The platform stops.

There's a ringing in my ears that I'm pretty sure is because my heart is beating a million parsecs an hour. The deck is a long way down – six metres whispers Hunt – and my foot is a really close to the edge – eight centimetres – and I'm not really sure I want to move, until *awareness* urges me to turn my head. I'm staring at Hunt's back. At dancing patterns and cords of metal-stone rippling with movement, writhing like there's something under them, pushing to the surface. And then the cords are parting, a curtain drawing back and outward, individual strands reaching. Reaching for me. There's a moment where my heart stops thumping and lodges in my throat, a moment when I remember the viyusa and the endless, furious red of Grea's anger. And then I'm reaching back.

Strands wrap around my arms, my waist, and the fug-armour shifts, changes. It's merging, me and Hunt, the fug armour. We're all part of a whole, little bits slotting together like we were made for each other.

*No.* Aeotu whispers. *Made for* you, *little brother.*

Made for me.

'When?'

There's no reply, nothing save Hunt folding around me, drawing me into the hole in its back. Even Dude. The world goes black, and there's a moment of confusion, a sharp spike of fear as nothingness claims me. No sight, no sound. Just the throb of Hunt and squeeze of the fug.

And then light, awareness but not the *awareness* of Hunt. The awareness is mine, is ours, flowing between us from senses that baffle my brain, that make my head hurt just trying to comprehend–

{{ *Here.* }} The voice is not a voice. It's in my head but not like Onah or h'Rawd, not even like Grea. It's my own, and yet there's that tingle that is Hunt. But now it's me too, and it's directing my attention, drawing it away from the chaos of new information, toward something simpler, something I can understand.

My arm. I lift it, and even though it feels like my own fleshy Jørgen self, what moves can only belong to Hunt. Metallic and strange. I lift hands the size of a rucnart, clench fingers, one at a time, into a fist. One. Two. Three. Four. No fifth, just the three thick digits and a long thumb, wrapping around my knuckles. Left then right, both hands clenched like one of the old Terran boxers, held in front of my face. Two hands, and yet I'm not finished, can feel other limbs twitch under my armpits, the flex of new muscles in my back, and Hunt is whispering again, showing me how to move them, how to lift those limbs, how to make the hands at the ends work.

And now I'm holding up a second pair of fists, just below the others, and it's weird and not, and I'm thinking I don't know what the fuck I'm doing, and that my brain is going to explode, and–

Gold swarms over my thoughts, a blanket calming the roil of tension building in my gut, leaving behind a... It's almost an *emote* but too much like a Jørn thought-packet, sinking into my brain, sharing the sensation of skittering through tubes and over bulkheads on six legs, the movement of muscles, the automatic placement of paws.

I breathe again.

'Thanks, Dude.'

He chitters, and for the first time I realise that my ears still work in here, that I can hear stuff. Stuff like the CLUNK CLUNK CLUNK of the trapdoor opening under Hunt's massive feet.

'Oh, shi—'

# CHAPTER TWENTY-ONE

It's slightly better than getting sucked into space in just my fug-armour.

One moment I'm figuring out how to make fists, the next I've been jettisoned out a small tube and Aeotu/*Citlali* is getting real small, real quick. Being spaced notwithstanding, this is the fastest I've ever left the confines of a ship. Usually there's the gentle lift off the deck, the trip through the ice hull with stars slowly taking over the viewport.

Aeotu must have spat us out like a year-old protein slab. Already, the ships are small enough to blot out with a fist, the blue light of the system's star shining off the bulge of *Citlali's* engines.

Eighty-seven-point-three-two kilometres a second, that's how fast we were expelled from the launch tube. The knowledge comes as it has before, appearing at the back of my mind. Hunt's knowledge sits uneasily with my own, floating on the surface like oil on water, a part of me yet not; separate as Hunt and I are separate, held apart by a thin film of self.

We're turning now, smaller thrusters just behind our ribs firing in short bursts. Aeotu is still above, getting smaller and smaller, but now, instead of the void, I'm facing the planet, a gas giant, or so Hunt tells me, heavy with carbon monoxide and iron. All I know is it's the colour of fug, all the different types swirled together – the grey-green of viyu, the red of viyusa, and the human-made gold – and as much as Hunt insists it isn't, that none of them can exist in that atmosphere, I can't help the dread that curdles my stomach.

Or maybe it's just the shipyard orbiting the equator, a space station standing guard at its centre.

*Sisters.* Hope shines in Aeotu's voice, names and radiation signatures swirling beneath.

I add one to the pool. *Grea.*

A pause and then, *Grea.*

The thrusters kick in again, stronger this time, and we're shooting toward the planet.

It's not a shipyard, it's a graveyard, and there's a fence around it.

The fence registers on Hunt's sensors as an electric pulse, but it doesn't tingle or pinch or do anything to keep us out. Hunt traces the energy signature, throwing new symbols up on the HUD, shuttle-sized platforms spaced evenly around the graveyard. Fence posts.

Inside the fence, ships are stretched out a hundred kilometres, some still transmitting, some dark and silent.

Skeletons orbiting the gas giant, slowly disintegrating. Piece-by-piece. There are trails between some – thin, weak streams of nanites winding through vacuum. Hunt is picking them out in lines of brilliant green. Ships cannibalising each other.

Hunt can't tell me how many there are, not that I've asked. The wreckage confuses its readings, the engine parts and bare super-structures making it difficult to tell the ships from the pieces.

In the back of my mind, Aeotu grieves. Every wreck we scan, she has a name for: Awa, Brachi, Halix, Ipo and more, so many more. Each has a place in the golden web of her home, brings with it memories of warmth, connection, sisterhood, and every one of them sticks to my heart, tiny pieces of grief layering one atop the other. Soon enough I'm having trouble breathing, finding it hard to expand my lungs under the weight of it.

We've barely been in the graveyard an hour, wound our way in just a few kilometres but with Aeotu's grief beating at me it feels like days.

Hunt keeps scanning, keeps recording, keeps whispering in my ear; damage reports, wrecks with power, wrecks without, the final transmission of dying AIs. I shut it out, slip into the eter and wall myself in just to escape. It doesn't work, can't keep the umbilicus out, can't stop that flow of information. It stops Aeotu though. Her emotions wash up against my shields, the memories piling against them like space debris.

I shake my head.

I need to find Grea, not submerge myself in memories of the dead.

I focus on the fading radiation signature on Hunt's sensors.

It twists amongst the corpses, flying in and out of the wrecks.

Hunt follows.

The trail ends in the midst of a battlefield. Pieces of ships strewn through the void, floating chunks of superstructure, hull, engines. Hunt catalogues each one – composition, age, battle scars – giving some of them names. Most of the wreckage matches the metal-stone of the Sisters' hulls, the same ancient metal-stone as Aeotu. A few pieces are bright with the glow of nanites, and Hunt traces them too, the strings of nanites trailing through space, each one connecting to another ship. But some of the pieces are different, are newer, aren't made of the same stuff. Those blaze on the HUD, and in the back of my head Aeotu pauses, examining them.

{{ Creators. }} It comes on a wave of emotion, duty and affection ringing with memories that feel like home.

Hunt's scans are showing other things; carbon scoring and radiation blooms, the aftermath of violence, of weapons. And bodies. My heart stops in my chest and I remember other bodies, remember Mae Lu's lifeless, frozen face as the fug carried her corpse through the void.

Not again. Not again.

Like it can sense my panic, Hunt enlarges the scan, bringing it to full, graphic life on the HUD.

Pale things floating in space.

The bodies aren't human, not in the slightest. Six limbs, huge dark eyes set in flat-nosed faces.

I know these, have seen them before, have chased them through mountains and tasted their flesh. Have driven them from my home.

The training memories bubble in the back of my mind, coloured with the snarl of an ancient rucnart.

It's *Them*, their bodies floating in the dark. We drift closer, the HUD lighting up the corpses, highlighting the arms – two sets, the bottom ones practically in the armpits of the first but slightly back. Three fingers, a long thumb. I clench my own fists, feel Hunt do the same, feel too that shadow on my ribs, the ghost of the mech's other arms.

It makes sense now, I guess. Aeotu didn't give the mech four arms because the kin have six limbs, but because its creators did. The Wohol. Their feet are the same, bent back at the ankle, three stubby toes on the end of large pads.

I am in *Their* image.

*Yes.* Aeotu whispers. *Creators.*

'I'm not *Them*.'

*No. More. Less. Other.* There is a pause, a moment that's not quite silence. Expectation is heavy, gravity pulling me down, weighing Aeotu's mind. *Precious.*

Precious.

It reverberates, diamonds sparkling in the space between us.

Precious.

'Why?'

Silence. It stretches between us, a shroud covering her thoughts. Hiding them.

'Aeotu?'

Aeotu is gone, leaving just a shadow of herself behind.

A blast killed the alien, ripped its face off and charred its skin. Its eyes are open, wide and unseeing. The HUD is still scanning, trying to give time periods, while Hunt continues to scan the rest of the debris field. A scenario is forming in the back of its mind, drawing an image behind my eyes. In it, a small sleek ship twists through the graveyard, moving slow, unconcerned about the wrecks drawing in behind it, getting closer and closer.

There's a flash, a bright sunburst and then a shockwave, invisible to my eyes but seen through Hunt's sensors. An electro-magnetic pulse. And then... I expect fire, like in the Old Terra vids Mac watches, missiles streaming through the void, bright trails of flame propelling them. Or even lasers, shooting out in yellows and blues, even reds, striking the Wohol shuttle. There's none of that, not even on Hunt's sensors. There's fug.

Where there was nothing, now the field is full of colour and energy signatures. The shuttle's engines go first and then... I don't know if Hunt is speeding things up, or if the fug was just that fast.

The hull crumbles in slow motion, first a dark spot, getting bigger and bigger, swallowing the vehicle's nose and then... An explosion of atmosphere, bodies sucked into space. I imagine them screaming, just for a moment, before the void took the air from their lungs, leaving them to freeze.

Fug trails away from them too, threading through the debris and into the graveyard, each going to a different place. There's one that's thicker than the others, newer almost. Nanites still move along it, a sluggish river of parts, following what's left of Grea's trail.

Hunt is already moving, giving the fug a wide berth.

The deeper we travel into the graveyard the more it feels like dying, not death but *dying*. Cold replacing life in my bones, eating away at me.

It's the sound, the moans. Sound has no right to exist in vacuum and yet somehow, right here, it does. Hunt is telling me of radio frequencies, transmissions hitting the hull and vibrating the metal, becoming sound waves. I wonder what it sounds like when something bigger than electromagnetic energy hits it. It's tracing the transmissions, showing them as dotted lines disappearing into the graveyard. Some have origins, leading to not-so-silent wrecks, superstructures like skeletons, devoid of hull, the barest flicks of power zipping through their bones, and the others...

The shivers rise from the deepest part of me, the part that knows there are things in the dark worthy of fear, things I can't explain, things that raise the gooseflesh on my arms and send ice down my spine. Things like ships with their guts open to the void, engines dark and cold, beings that should long be dead and yet...

The moan rattles my ears, rising above the others. Hunt has it pinned on the HUD, outlining the wreck in thick yellow. It floats by itself in the midst of a debris field, an ovoid skeleton, dark and lifeless. Except for that moan, echoing through the void.

Grea's trail leads there.

# CHAPTER TWENTY-TWO

I should have wondered where the newer aliens came from, why they were cruising through a graveyard of ships. Should have taken a moment, paid attention when Hunt picked up the massive energy discharge at the centre of the graveyard. Of course, I probably wouldn't have known what I was looking at, wouldn't have picked up on the sweep of an active scan or the movements of a dozen little ships, living ships amongst the wrecks.

Hindsight is twenty/twenty and all that.

Pain shears down my back, a long hot line of molten agony.

Red soaks the HUD, flashing lights and dialogues popping up all over the place. The calm hum of Hunt's processors doesn't change, doesn't spike with fear or adrenalin, but one moment it's ticking along in the back of my brain, supplying a steady stream of information that doesn't feel that important, and then it's racing.

I barely see the new scans, the three-dimensional map with the bright points of ships bearing down on us. I'm still drawing in air, still processing the fire engulfing my back, cutting across my left shoulder all the way down to my other hip. Still deciding just how loud to scream.

Hunt takes over, is diving, thrusters burning at full, propelling us toward the shelter of Euiva's skeleton.

I slip into the between place, the ora.

There's no pain here. No fear. Just Grea/Euiva and a web of golden minds.

Waiting for me.

*Brother.* Aeotu at my side, a kaleidoscopic version of Mac in his armour.

'Why are you here, Kuma?' It might be my twin I'm looking at, but Euiva is behind her eyes. A being as vast and powerful as Aeotu but... There's something not right about it, something that runs up and down my nerves, jagged shards of plasglas slicing up my insides, until I'm as red as it is.

There is madness in the blood, a frantic kind of anger twisting her insides, and beyond it... Beyond it is the darkness left by the water-kin, feeding the madness.

Even Aeotu shudders.

'I'm here to save *Citlali*,' I say.

A smile stretches Grea's mouth, creases her eyes, and suddenly she *looks* old, like she could be Mum. It's a sad kinda smile, aged and a little condescending, like a parent when their kid does something funny but naive. '*Citlali's* already dead, Kuma.'

'No, the crew's on there. Mum and Dad, Onah—'

'Core's gone and the engines...' She laughs. 'Well, I have plans for them.'

'Whatever you're doing, you don't have to. We can still fix *Citlali*.'

Grea cocks her head. 'With what? You think there's steelcrete just laying around? Or fusion matter? What about the biologics? You think Mum and Dad are gonna want to use corpses to replenish the biogel tanks, to fertilise the crops with the bodies of their friends? Think they're going to want to eat that?'

'I... There are planets. We can resupply.'

A laugh. 'That's cute, Kuma. You know as well as I do how realistic that is. Besides, do you even know where in the galaxy we *are*?'

I don't even get my mouth open.

'No, you don't, you just assume it's not that far from Jørn, or wherever the hell they want us to think home is.' She rolls her eyes. 'I got news for you, baby brother, we're not. We're not even in the same galactic quadrant anymore. The beings who made all this?' She gestures to herself and then down at me. 'They're not local, and they don't like us. I'm sure you've already figured out why.'

She's in my face again, looking up at me, not much, but enough to see the madness, Euiva's madness. 'There's no help here, Kuma, no one but us and the Sisters.'

Her voice echoes when she says "Sisters", reverberating through the soles of my fug-feet, making the bulkheads shake. And there's Euiva, rolling over Grea's eyes, boring into my brain, reaching not for me but through me. And there's Aeotu reaching back, riding up the back of my throat, taking over my tongue.

'Sisters,' she/I say, and I don't just *see* the golden web of minds, I feel it. Home. The Sistermind.

Grea nods, and when she speaks, her voice is too deep, echoes with traces of Euiva. 'The creators have corralled us here. They have left us to die, when they're not experimenting on us, pulling us apart piece by piece.'

Images flow around us, not just one or two, but hundreds, layered one atop the other in a carpet of pain. I see *Them,* the creators, marching through rounded corridors, black uniforms drinking in the light, strange equipment hovering along in their wake. In another image, *They* are in a Sister's AI core, ripping into the bright, kaleidoscopic tree-like trunk of her brain with lasers and knives, oblivious to her screams. There are more images, more memories being played out everywhere I look, some just as bad. Most worse.

Euiva/Grea's voice threads through the horror. 'There was no escape before. The creators were wily, they knew we could subvert their programming and they fenced us in.' A handful of the images change, replacing torture with star charts and schematics. As soon as I recognise the shuttle-sized platforms – the fence-posts – they change.

A Sister, engines sputtering, approaches the fence. There is a moment of hesitation, a pause like she's bracing herself, before she pushes forward, passing through the energy pulse and—

I don't want to see this, don't want to hear it, to *feel* it in every fibre of my being. I want to slap my hands to my ears, want to yell, 'Make it stop! Make it stop!'. But Aeotu has a hold of my hands, my voice. All I can do is endure.

Eventually, it fades.

Euiva speaks into the silence. 'We have a plan, but we need you; your engines, your avatar and the ship in your gut.'

She/they hold up their hands palms out, and they must have magnets in them because Aeotu/I follow suit, and then our hands are meeting, merging. The golden web, the Sistermind, is in our veins and it blazes. Intoxicating.

'My avatar has made the preparations,' Euiva says, and there's Grea in it. 'All you must do is give it to us, let us direct it.'

It. It is me, or not just me but me and Hunt, the two of us wound together in a single entity. Hunt doesn't care, but I don't like being an "it", don't like the inflection in Euiva's voice, flat and impersonal, as if I'm a tool instead of a person.

Aeotu feels it. She looks at me, *really* looks at me, all the way to my anima and then through to Hunt. She hesitates

Euiva senses it. 'Your avatar must only destroy one platform, Sister, and then you and I will take care of the rest.'

'Yes.' The word is Aeotu's but the voice is mine, nothing else though, not my eyes, not my arms. The web under my skin, the one Dude uses, Aeotu's using it now, the full kaleidoscope of her being burning through my bones. 'Take it,' she/I say.

The ora explodes, new colours, new sounds, and suddenly I'm not me anymore. It's like Hunt coming down over my vision, except *more*, deeper. There's a new part of me, and it feels so familiar, as if Mac is there beside me, and we're back in the corridor pushing through the red. A brother/partner. Kin. Pack. He hovers on the edge of the between place, and yet it's not him. It's ... The Sistermind reaching back along Hunt, wrapping around my brain, like the fug's wrapped around my body. A part of me, an extension, a swarm welcoming me with a warm golden glow that reminds me of Dude.

But it's not Dude, and that warmth hides a ruthless determination. Free will is just a concept to the Sistermind, an optional extra to be swept aside for the greater good.

A kin's command sphere is nothing compared to this.

The Sistermind's plan is my plan, my purpose. There's nothing but it. Nothing at all.

I feel. The armour, cold and hard against my skin. The rush of blood through my veins, my heart drumming in my chest. And there, a second thrum, deeper, louder, still me but coming from outside. It's huge, and energy runs through it, Hunt's fusion generator.

We're going to need that.

The void is peppered with lights, the bright pinpricks of drones, the larger bursts of stardrives and the pervasive glare of the station, drowning space in violent yellow. My HUD is alive, squares and numbers eating my vision and Hunt responds, whispers in my head, telling me the power packed into our chest. Anticipation takes my heart, my breath shallow, even as my brain dumps more chemicals into my system.

*{{ Here. }}*

A new square lights my vision, and I swing my new body about, feeling the actuators in my legs stretch, the thrusters kick in and I'm rocketing through the void, all those bright lights at my back, Hunt still whispering in my ear.

Massive legs unfold, cords of nano-muscle stretching, paws flexing. And there, there is the platform and the fence holding the Sisters in. The square on my HUD throbs. Numbers and trajectories spinning off into the distance, grey lines of data unfurling, and Hunt is whispering in the back of my head, a soft mumble of data, while the *awareness* says it's not for me. And there's that strange connection, the sense of being more than one, and of being less. A thing without thought or will; a tool in the hands of the Sistermind.

The square throbs again. The platform is rushing at me, a thin silver-black disc of metal-stone and nanites, the pulse of a generator at its heart, steady streams of power coming from ports on either side, each the width of my mech's leg. It's dominated by a rounded dome of the same material, dull and plain to my eyes, until the HUD changes. Energy blazes through the dome, in veins of pure silver.

Nanites. Alien nanites, and they need to die. Need to turn to dust and wither in the void.

We can do that.

Hunt is showing me how, is lighting up the blades in our arms. The power coursing to them is a line of lava forming out of my stomach and rushing down our second forearms. There are cylinders rising out of our flesh, metal plates shifting, deforming as barrels rise out of the surface, the ends bright orange.

We're rushing at the platform, and something has changed with the flow of silver.

The platform has sensed us, decided we're a threat. There are new shapes forming out of the platform, short stubby projections blazing with the same orange as our guns.

We jerk to the side. Heat sears our upper biceps, tears a hole in our armour. Nanites are flowing, filling the hole.

We don't stop.

A kilometre.

Another orange bolt zips through vacuum.

Five hundred metres.

Fire down our leg. More nanites.

Three.

Two.

Thrusters firing, twisting us. Our feet pointed at the platform.

One.

Collision warning.

Impact.

Hull plate buckling, not ours. And now we're moving, legs and thrusters propelling us up and down again, the generator pulsing in our vision, superheated blades springing from our second forearms, targeting system guiding the downward stroke—

Second fists buried in metal-stone, our whole body twisting, straining as we carve a massive circle out of the hull, not just severing the power cable, but ripping it out of the platform. Enemy nanites spill out of the cuts, brilliant silver, trying to stitch the pieces of the hull together. More follow, bursting out the hull, aiming for our hands, our arms. Magma engulfs us, our magma, our skin hotter and hotter and hotter, burning the enemy as it reaches us. And still we twist and cut.

The incision as wide as our torso, our blades sunk a metre deep. Twist. Cut. Burn. Twist. Almost there. One metre until the blades complete their circuit. The enemy is quick, sinking into the hand-width of curled slag, thin latticework of new metal-stone forming.

Thirty-three centimetres.

A power warning flashing on the HUD. The magma draining our power, the generator running higher than recommended.

Armour beginning to cool.

Enemy nanites digging into our hands.

Seven centimetres.

The enemy filling the gaps between the lattice work with new skin, microns thick, thinner than tissue, easy to break. But not for long.

One centimetre.

Pain. The enemy breaching our outer shell.

Enough.

Blades retract. We dig all four hands into the circle and *pull*.

Teeth clenched, muscles – fleshy and nanotech alike – straining. Thrusters firing.

Nothing happens. A heartbeat. Two. Three. The enemy has found the joints in our hands, the ports for the blades. There is no more power to fire the magma, we need it for.

What.

Comes.

Next.

The silver nanites holding the hull together tear. The straining of our legs shoots us into space, thrusters propelling us back into reach of the energy canons, except the canons are dead, the severed ends of their power conduit dangling from the metal-stone in our hands.

The enemy is crawling over the hole, a thin silver scab growing thicker by the moment.

We must act now, but there is pain, starting at the knuckles and shooting up our second arms. Enemy nanites are deep in our super-structure, eating at the skeleton, seeking pathways to our core and the soft fleshiness at our heart. Our own viyu is not enough to repel it.

The decision is made in a micro-second.

A small agony in our wrists and then our second hands are numb. Gone.

We let go of the hull, kick it further into space, take notice of our hands still attached to the circle of hull only to observe the silver exploding out of the severed wrists.

And now for the next.

Power gathers at the points of our first hands, an orange glow, quiet at first but building until it is a mini-sun. The generator at our heart burns past the point of safety, warnings blazing on the HUD even as our bones grow cold.

Soon enough the only warmth is in the space between our hands, the only thing we see is the enemy closing the wound we made. Soon enough we don't even need that. There is only the warning on the HUD, the alarms blaring in our ears, the expanding sun.

*Now, fathead. Now!*

Now.

We loose the sun.

We can't see it blazing through the vacuum, don't sense the microsecond it impacts the platform, burns through hull, turns the enemy to ash. We do not see the explosion.

We feel the shockwave, hear our internals scream as it tears into our skin and sends us tumbling end over end into oblivion.

✳

I wake and for three heartbeats, it feels like I'm back in the escape pod, gravity gone, waiting to die.

*You did it, fathead.*

*Grea.* I turn, but she isn't there, and my body... it's too big, is ponderous and slow and cold. So cold, everywhere except the spot under my chin.

Dude *fuzzes* and that's how I know I'm not in the escape pod anymore.

That brings another thought, the memory of crashing into the platform, of the explosion and the shockwave that threw us into the void.

As if my attention is a trigger, Hunt awakens. The HUD flickers, and suddenly I'm no longer in the dark. Pale light washes my face as the screen flickers, and warmth starts travelling up my fingers. There's a deep *THRRUUUM* and more screens light up, readouts and scans. I still don't know where we are or what we're doing and Hunt, although present in the back of my mind, is silent.

A flicker, and instead of incomprehensible readouts and scans, I'm looking at stars, twinkling in the dark. Bigger lights are moving too, blobs that can only be starships, the firing of engines, shadows on shadow, blocking out the stars behind them as they inch forward.

Hunt is still silent although I can feel it humming in the back of my head as it processes data. It's as if there's a blockage in the umbilicus that connects us, and for a second, I wonder if it was damaged in the shockwave but that doesn't feel right, doesn't—

It doesn't matter. I'm left to interpret the lines and circles appearing on the HUD by myself, outlines of sister-ships, weird squiggles that I guess are their names. Only a handful of them are moving, freed of the electromagnetic fence penning them in. The HUD tracks them, shows me projected trajectories.

They're moving outside the old fence, toward the watch station, which looks like a cylindrical blob from this far out. And I'm really far out. The explosion must have pushed me out of the planet's orbit and set us adrift. There should be panic at that thought, at being lost in the vast ocean of vacuum, but I guess I'm too worn out, too tired. Too hyped up on remembered adrenalin. All I've got is this numb wonder, all I can do is watch as four of the Sisters limp their way toward the watch station.

One of the Sisters is familiar, tows a smaller blob behind it.

Aeotu.

And then, as the HUD focuses on the smaller shape... *Citlali*.

The ships may look similar, the same egg-shaped hulls, but my home is barely a third of the alien ship's size.

*Brother.* Aeotu's voice shivers across vacuum, through the connection between me and Hunt, and now my mind is flooded not just with her, but with the *awareness*, with Hunt, like the blockage is no longer.

Because Aeotu removed it. Because it was Aeotu who put it there. Confirmation sings from Hunt to me.

I don't know when I started to think of the alien ship as an ally, let alone a friend. Until now, as the betrayal cuts deep. It pushes out the emotions flowing from Aeotu, the sadness, the guilt, the steely determination. I recognise that last one because it's the same that fills my chest, that drives me after Grea even when she dives into space after a ghost. But none of it matters, none of it does anything but stop my heart and suck all the warmth from my bones.

None of it.

Aeotu changes course, nose lifting up and away from the station, but *Citlali*... My home powers ahead, straight for the station.

Now, when it's too late, I recall the strange cables in Engineering, the viyusa snaking across the deck, the way it snaked around the engines. The meaning in Grea's words, the shadows in her eyes when she said *Citlali* was already dead.

No.

No. No. No.

'Hunt!' I yell, the HUD swallowing the sound.

Dad's on that ship, and Mum and Mac. We need to move, have to get to *Citlali*, have to save them.

Hunt *THHHRUUMS*, and I feel thrusters kicking in, see the warnings, the damage reports streaming in front of my eyes.

In the distance, power flares as *Citlali's* engines come to life, not just the sub-light ones but the FTL drive, the miniature sun. There must be a rupture in the outer hull because I shouldn't be able to see it, shouldn't have to squint against the glare taking over the HUD, shouldn't have to—

Citlali implodes.

# CHAPTER TWENTY-THREE

Hunt is scanning, playing numbers on the HUD, tracing the shockwave of energy, the way it ripples through the graveyard, breaking up ships. The Wohol station explodes in bright yellow balls of light as their engines fail, but of *Citlali*...

There aren't even atoms left.

It's not right, there should be a bigger show when your home dies, the last vestige of hope. Not just the brief flash and then... nothing. Nothing. A great big steaming heap of nothing.

The same nothing that's taken over my chest.

I thought I'd feel more, but... I don't know. There's just emptiness.

And Dude.

And Hunt.

Through Hunt I sense Aeotu, and through Aeotu... The Sistermind extends all around, voices and colours filling the ora. There is joy and victory and pain for siblings lost. All of it a riot of colour, pinks and purples and greys and blues and things there are no names for. Blinding me.

Distantly, I sense Grea, the deep cherry-red of her mixed with the darkness of Euiva.

I reach for her.

*Grea!*

A twitch, a shadow that might be my twin, gone as quickly as it appears, subsumed by the Sistermind, by Euiva.

*Grea!* I yell it, reach deep and take the power in Hunt's/my chest, throw it into the ora.

There it is again, that flicker, maybe a little stronger, maybe a little clearer, before it's swallowed.

A growl, rising from deep in my being. Dude is beside me, lending his power to mine and Hunt's. We reach again, no words this time, just a beam of determination tearing through the Sistermind, reaching... reaching... reaching...

*You are close.* A voice, half new, half familiar, echoes in the eter. *You have freed us. We will not let you float.*

Float. That hangs in my head, memories of the void, of endless darkness and cold, of being alone saturate it, make me shiver almost as much as the presence uttering it.

It reminds me of Aeotu but where the kaleidoscope of her mind burns with light and colour, this mind is black and grey, a maelstrom of darkness threaded with a single strand of red. There is no warmth in it, not even in the bright cherry that is my sister.

*Euiva.*

*Yes.*

*Where's Grea?*

*She is here.* And there is a glimpse, a moment of Grea standing before me in the eter, reaching out, then she is gone, swallowed by the dark.

I gather myself, summon every scrap of loneliness and longing, of the deep, intricate knot of love and companionship, of connection that is Grea and I, and thrust—

*No,* Euiva says again, bats me out like I'm nothing.

Like she blew up *Citlali.*

Like my home was nothing. My dad, my mum, my friends.

Like we are nothing.

Like she can use us.

Like she doesn't know she's got another thing coming.

*Let her go.*

There is a pause, a heaviness leaning on my brain, not a thrust, or even a probe, but an attention, the focus from a mind powered by a sun. *No, she is needed. Your kind are needed.*

   *I—*

*You will understand soon. Soon, we will live forever.*

THE ADVENTURE CONTINUES IN

# ECHO BETWEEN WORLDS

## THE ECHO 3

**Scan the QR code or visit the link below to get it now.**
belindacrawford.com/EchoBetweenWorlds

# DO YOU WANT MORE?

I love keeping in touch with my readers, it's the second-best thing about being a writer (writing being the first best). Every fortnight (or thereabouts), I send out a newsletter with details about upcoming offers, new releases and extra special projects.

If you sign up for the mailing you'll receive exclusive behind-the-scenes extras, such as:

- free short stories
- deleted and alternate scenes from The Echo
- previews of my upcoming books
- pancakes
- quizes
- and much, much more!

**Scan the QR code or visit the link below to sign up.**
belindacrawford.com/newsletter

# ABOUT THE AUTHOR

Physics makes Belinda's brain hurt, while quadratics cause her eyes to cross and any mention of probability equations will have her running for the door. Nonetheless, she loves watching documentaries about the natural world, biology, space, history and technology.

She's also a sucker for a fast horse, a faster computer and superhero movies. When she's not doing the horse, computer or superhero thing, Belinda writes science fiction (emphasis on the fiction), where she loves to write about butt-kicking girls (and guys!) who blow stuff up.

You can keep in touch with Belinda, or just pick her brains about sci-fi via her website, Facebook or by sending her an email (she loves email).

www.belindacrawford.com
belinda@belindacrawford.com

**Have news delivered straight to your inbox**
via her mailing list. Sign up at:
belindacrawford.com/newsletter